Chance Meeting

Finally. Laurie couldn't have waited much longer for him to leave the phone booth. She had to make a call. But instead of leaving, he kissed her and asked her to go home with him.

Laurie pulled away, shaking her head but grinning at him anyway because she was pleased with the flattery. She fished for an excuse. "I'm with friends."

"Can't I be your friend?"

"Sure, but I can't go with you, really. . . ."

He wouldn't accept her refusal. He looked at her for a moment and then pulling her with him into the alcove kissed her again in a way that made clear he was dead serious. Then he let go of her. "I'll be at the bar," he said, "and I'll be waiting there forever for you."

Hettie Jones

You Light Up My Life

PUBLISHED BY POCKET BOOKS NEW YORK

Another *Original* publication of POCKET BOOKS

POCKET BOOKS, a Simon & Schuster division of
GULF & WESTERN CORPORATION
1230 Avenue of the Americas, New York, N.Y. 10020

ISBN: 0-671-82512-7

First Pocket Books printing January, 1979

10 9 8 7 6 5 4 3 2 1

Trademarks registered in the United States and other countries.

Printed in the U.S.A.

You Light Up My Life

1.

"That's why you get more for your money with Fenwick Farm Fresh Eggs."

No, that was wrong. It was Fenwick *Fresh Farm* Eggs. Laurie closed her eyes and rested her head on the steering wheel, her hair over her face like a dark brown curtain. There was too much on her mind. The song she was writing was spoiling her concentration. Its half-formed melody seemed to lurk at the edge of every conscious thought. But music wasn't earning her living. She reached for the script. You had to get the words right when you read for a TV commercial or you didn't get the part.

The light changed; horns blew before she could start. The little red car was old and had no pick-up. *Maybe Kenny's right*, Laurie thought. *I should let him get me a new one after we're mar-*

ried. Except she loved this vintage convertible with the strips of adhesive tape that held its roof together. "Nice car," she said, patting the dashboard. Her father had taught her never to malign old cars lest they get insulted and malfunction. And she wasn't married yet. Not until Sunday. Today was only Tuseday.

But she wasn't concentrating on the work. Hollywood Boulevard stretched out before her in the late morning haze. She drove holding the script in one hand. "That's why you get more for your money with Fenwick Fresh Farm Eggs," she said cheerfully. *"Fresh Farm Eggs."* A woman passenger in the car beside her stared at her moving mouth. "You see," Laurie said, looking right at her. "Not all eggs are the same." She flashed the astonished woman a smile as she turned into the ad agency's parking lot.

The main audition room was on the twentieth floor. The director was late. Laurie waited near the reception desk, staring out a picture window that overlooked the Hollywood Hills. Funny how they never impressed her: every time she gave the California landscape any thought she rediscovered her yearning to go back East. The mountains of her childhood superimposed themselves on the scene outside. The freeway faded and the neat bungalow colonies returned, surrounded by pine forest, birch in the distance. The Catskills, New York. The music began again in her head, two clear bars surfaced, a ballad in three-quarter time:

It's the morning of my life
I want to write you a song
It's the start of something nice
And so I'll write you a song. . . . *

"Jim's here, he'll see you now, Miss Robinson."
The receptionist's lashes fluttered rapidly behind
her large glasses. Laurie thanked her, struggling
to banish the song from her brain, then shoul-
dered her heavy bag and went inside.

Jim Hall took his job seriously, and he had seen
a lot of actresses. Laurie was good, he thought,
if she could only keep her mind on it. He sat with
his head cocked to one side, regarding her while
she read for him as though she were one-half
woman and one-half performing seal.

"You see not all eggs are the same," she said
without conviction. "We send our hens high into
the hills . . . and the special grass we feed them
. . . and the tranquil life . . . produce larger eggs.
The larger the egg, the fluffier the omelet . . ."
What stupid crap. She looked at Jim despairingly.
How could she do this?

He got up from his desk and put an arm around
her. "No, no, no," he said with the exaggerated
kindness people usually reserve for children.
"You're speaking to these housewives as if they're
dummies. That's wrong. They won't like it. You
want to *befriend* them. You want to say: 'I've
been where you're at. I too have had flat, uneven

---

omelets. But now . . . I've seen the light.' " He smiled encouragingly at Laurie. "Understand?"

"Uh . . . no." She couldn't help saying it. The idea was just too stupid.

"No," he repeated, his disbelief evident. How could she not understand something so simple? Wasn't she well? He stared at her, but she was serious. "Ah, well, okay," he said. "Ah, okay, honey—I've got it. It's as if I take off this watch . . . and give it to you . . ." He slipped his watch onto her wrist. "And you say 'Thank you, Jim . . .'

"Well, *they* all say—all the housewives, you know?—they all say 'thank you, Laurie Robinson, for telling us about Fenwick Fresh Farm Eggs.' Can you read it like that?"

"I don't know, I—" Laurie began to want out. "I don't think—" It was useless, she just didn't feel like doing this audition. Maybe better to just leave right now.

"Oh you can do it, Laurie," Jim said. "He wanted to fuss at her but made an effort not to let his exasperation show through and rattle her completely. What was wrong with her this morning? "C'mon, we'll go inside now, they're ready to shoot. C'mon, keep your energy up, it'll be terrific." He knew he didn't sound convinced but at least he was trying. *These girls,* he thought, *so damn touchy . . .*

They walked across the hall to the audition room where the ad men were waiting. There were three of them plus a woman, all even more serious than Jim.

10

"Ah, gentlemen, we meet again," Jim said. "This is Laurie Robinson."

They nodded and took sips of their coffee; no one smiled. Laurie smiled anyway and said hello, hoping to charm them, or if not, merely to loosen them up. *What an audience*, she thought. They were not only deadpan but stiff, waiting for something to happen.

"Ok, roll 'em," Jim called to the cameraman. "Action."

"Laurie Robinson, Conway Agency, Take One," Laurie said brightly, trying to warm up to it. "Fenwick hens are *happy* hens. Week after week, month after month, finer eggs for fluffier omelets . . . We send our hens high into the hills . . ."

"Cut," Jim said. "Too much emotion."

"Jim, I think perhaps I can help . . ." It was one of the ad men, the creative director. He stepped forward toward Laurie.

Jim blocked his way. "No, Bob, let me just work with her on another point."

But the creative director would have his say. "Well you see it's all wrong." He walked around Jim and confronted Laurie. Bob was a mousy man and smelled vaguely of a fake woodsy perfume she had always hated. "You see, I'd like you to see this as an egg," he said, holding his hand out.

"What?" Laurie stared at the pink, fleshy object that emerged from his sleeve.

"An egg. You know, just sort of picture an egg there in the palm of my hand. You see, I think you're seeing it as the end product . . . I think you're seeing it as the omelet. But I see it as the egg."

"Ah yes, exactly!" Jim exclaimed. "Exactly—the egg . . . absolutely!" He beamed at the creative director, who took the compliment with a modest nod.

Laurie looked from one to the other. "I don't know what the hell you guys are talking about," she said. It came out before she could stop herself. She was shocked at her nerve. She'd never said such a thing before at an audition.

Jim pulled her aside. "Look, Laurie, you've got to talk to these housewives as if they're one person. Listen . . ." His voice became a conspiratorial whisper. "When you were little, you were always the first to do everything. And you'd show your best friend the way. So you see, it's as if you sent away for the *decoder ring*, and then she sent away for the decoder ring. And yours came in the mail but she never got hers. So you ask her, 'Did you remember to include your return address?' and she thinks, and then she says 'No.' And you say 'No? Well, no *wonder* you're having trouble making fluffy omelets!—' Get it?"

Laurie, who as a child had never sent away for anything because her return address was rarely the same from one week to the next, found it hard to project herself into the situation. "I see," she said, although she really didn't. "What you're saying is I want to help these people?"

"No, you want to help their *omelets*."

"Oh. I want to help their *omelets*."

"Exactly." He beamed. "Can you pick up right from there?"

"Okay." Laurie sighed, watching one of the ad men suppress a yawn. "Okay, this is a Fenwick egg." She held up her script, balancing an imaginary egg. This had better be good, she warned herself. She needed the work. She began to concentrate.

"Wait—you didn't give me a slate." It was the technician, a woman with sharp red nails and hair to match.

Laurie felt as if someone had stuck a pin in her. "I gave you a slate before," she said.

"Better give us another."

Laurie knew better than to argue with her. "Laurie Robinson, Conway Agency, continuing Take One." She took a breath, then went on: "This is a Fenwick egg. This is a regular egg. Notice the difference? After you've tried a Fenwick egg, you'll say, 'No *wonder* I've been having trouble making fluffy omelets.'"

"Cut." Jim started toward her.

But Bob was already there. "You see," he said, "the whole idea here . . . is that because Fenwick hens are happy hens, they lay bigger eggs. And the bigger the egg, the fluffier the omelet." His smile was radiant with belief in his mission; he was going to convert her.

"You know, that's really not true," Laurie said defensively. "It's not the egg that makes the omelet fluff, it's the milk."

13

"What?" Jim could hardly believe his ears. What the hell could be wrong with her?

"It's the milk," Laurie repeated stubbornly, into the dead silence.

"Are we gonna do this again?" the technician asked, her nails clutching a reel of tape.

"No, I think that's enough," Jim said, rather sadly. He turned to the others. "Don't you?"

In unison they nodded, their loosened ties flapping, their cardboard coffee containers dipping and flashing.

"Thank you, Laurie," Jim said.

"Yes, thanks very much." The creative director gave her a fast false smile.

"Thank you," Laurie said automatically, then realized as she turned to leave that she meant it. *Thank you, I didn't want to do it anyway, it's too damn stupid and it's a lie.*

"Don't forget your bag," Jim said. He held it out to her. *Maybe she's sick, poor kid,* he thought. She sure looked confused.

"Oh, thanks." Laurie took the bag from him and started for the door.

"Uh, Laurie, uh . . . "

"Yes?" She turned back.

"You still have my watch."

She looked at her wrist. "Oh, sorry, Jim, here . . . " Laurie pulled off the watch and fled. To hell with Fenwick eggs.

2.

Kenny was already halfway through his steak sandwich when Laurie managed to shove her way through the lunchtime crowd at Vernon's. He had a mouthful so she kissed his ear just below the black line of his curls, which she knew made him shiver and embarrassed him terribly. But it was compensation for her being late, and besides, shivering made him even handsomer. Ken had been voted Best Looking and Best Athlete in their high school class, Laurie the Most Talented. They had been lumped together as the two most out-standing students so often that it seemed natural they should also eventually fall in love and get married.

"Hi, honey," he said when he finally swallowed. Kenny waved a hand at Vernon behind the counter. "Another steak sandwich, please—plain, with nothing on it." Then he turned to Laurie. "That's your steak sandwich I just ordered."

"How come?" She frowned.

"That other stuff you eat makes me sick."

At the moment Laurie was a vegetarian. She took a deep breath and somehow in the mad rush caught Vernon's eye. "Oh Vern, listen, I'd rather just have a taco with refried beans and a pickle." It was a plea. She didn't want to have an argument. *Please no arguments, Kenny,* she thought, *not after Fenwick Farms.*

He turned to her, chewing hard again. "Michael and Connie asked us over for cocktails later today."

"I can't go."

"Why not?"

She could tell he was angry. "Because I have a recording session later." Vern brought her taco and Laurie, feeling guilty, busied herself with hot sauce and onion. This was the third time in less than two weeks that she had refused to go somewhere with him.

"Can't you cancel it?" Kenny stopped eating and looked at her. Lately she seemed always preoccupied and he guessed she was nervous about the wedding. He himself wasn't at all nervous, since he didn't expect that anything about his life would change after they were married.

"I can't cancel a session, Kenny," Laurie said. "I already booked the muscians and gave the studio a deposit."

"I'll give you back the money if you cancel it,"

16

he bargained. He hated going alone to places where everyone expected her to show up too. It implied there was trouble between them. "And why don't you let me pay for that stuff anyway?" he added irritably. It was a sore point that she never let him spend money on her, although he had plenty.

"Why do you keep calling it *stuff*? It's not *stuff*, it's a session," Laurie corrected, trying to remain patient.

"Whatever it is, this is the first time I knew you were paying for it."

"Well, who did you *think* was paying for it?" she exploded. "The Salvation Army? You're not the only one who earns money, you know."

"Take it easy, Laurie, will you?" He looked at the circles under her angry brown eyes. *She must be tired,* he thought, not without tenderness. *She's trying to do too much.* But he didn't know how to stop her. In fact, he wouldn't have dared try, because Laurie was so willful. Besides, she had always worked hard, working was a big part of her life.

Feeling his solicitude Laurie calmed down. *Poor Kenny,* she thought, *he always gets it from me and he doesn't deserve it.* She laid her hand on the strong muscular forearm, the tennis arm that had won him accolades and his current job as a pro. "Kenny, listen. I'll pay for my own sessions, it's better that way. But I appreciate the offer."

"It's okay." He nodded. "So what do we do about later?"

"I'm going to be recording later."

He looked at her and shrugged.

"I'm getting close to something, I can feel it in the music, Kenny, I know it. I can really sense it."

"Well, I'm going to Michael and Connie's."

"I think you *should* go," she said, anxious not to deprive him of a good time. "You always have fun with them."

"I don't see the big deal in canceling one lousy recording session," Kenny said, making one last stab at it.

One lousy recording session. Laurie could feel herself getting terribly, viciously angry. She wanted to scream but took a deep breath instead. He didn't mean it, she knew. "Listen, let's just drop the subject," she said evenly. "How was your morning?"

"Boring," he said with disgust. "Mornings are always boring when you have to teach beginners. But this afternoon I'm going to volley with Hampton Cook. How about that? He made it to the quarter finals in Southampton last year."

"That's great, Kenny—you'll really get a workout," Laurie felt relieved to have something positive to say.

"I know, I'm really looking forward to it." Tennis never failed to turn him on.

Laurie looked at the clock. She was going to be late for the Kiddie Komedy taping. "I gotta go, thanks for lunch, honey."

Kenny was eating another steak sandwich and

his mind was already on Hampton Cook's backhand. "Sure," he said. "I'll call you later."

"Have a good afternoon." Laurie kissed his cheek because he was chewing again. It occurred to her that they hadn't really kissed for days.

"I'll talk to you later," he said.

"Kenny, tell me," she whispered suddenly.

"Tell you what?" Starting with his mother, women had always mystified him.

"You know—break a leg."

"Oh yeah, yeah." These show-biz people with their weird customs. Her *and* her father. "Break a leg," he said dutifully. "Bye."

"Bye." Out of the corner of her eye Laurie saw him still shaking his head and chewing as she fled to the parking lot. *Dear Kenny,* she thought.

She had never quite understood why he loved her.

3.

She had four minutes to go on and as usual Si was making her nervous. He had always made her nervous before showtime. No matter where they played—in the comfortable air-conditioned dressing rooms of big hotels or in the makeshift facilities of seedy lodges—he would be there. In his undershirt, fretting. Sweating. Maybe it was because he'd always know her heart wasn't in it.

Now he paced the floor while she climbed into her overalls, slapped on some make-up, and fixed her hair in two pigtails. The costume as well as the role had been left by the previous star of the Kiddy Komedy Hour, whom she had replaced for the last two shows.

Laurie thought the whole attempt was ridiculous. The kids in the audience were all around three or four years old this week, too young for her material (Si's material really). She knew the act was going to bomb again. She pulled Larry the Dummy out of her bag. He was her third Larry the Dummy in fifteen years of performing. She didn't hate this one as much as the others. The first had terrified her, for when she was young the dummy had been real to her, and she had always suspected he understood the bad jokes made at his expense.

"Break a leg, sweetheart," Si whispered.

Laurie thought briefly of Ken, but then took a deep breath and strode onstage. "Hi everybody! My name is Laurie, and this here is Larry! Isn't he cute?"

The expected applause didn't materialize but Laurie picked up quickly. "Don't applaud too loud or he'll start asking me for food!"

No response. She sat down on the stool just to do something and to check out the kids. She focused on one of the oldest. "No—seriously, he loves you—he'd be smiling now, but last week we were a little short of cash, so I had to sell his teeth!"

The kid stared as though she had come from the moon. Laurie risked a quick glance at Tom, the director. He signaled her to keep going.

"He's a very smart kid though, this Larry. We had him tested, and you know what? He's only ten years old, but he has the brain of a thirty-year-old——monkey!"

Vacant looks. Silence. Why had Si insisted on this? Because Tom was his friend?

"Pablum—valium . . . " came Si's whisper from the wings.

"Jeez—you kids are wrecking my career," Laurie said, picking up the cue. "I didn't know pablum had valium in it these days!"

If anything, that was worse. Two kids looked at each other and shrugged. She wished Si would shut up.

"All joking aside though, this kid here really brightens up the house—he never turns off a light!"

In the silence Laurie spotted one kid smiling at her. Finally! She got up and went to him, looked in his ear. "Am I talking too fast for you kid? Hey—lemme take a look at you for a minute— Holy Toledo! I've discovered wax! Hey kid, you've got enough in there to record 'Oklahoma'!"

Tom was signaling for her to wind it up. There hadn't been even one decent laugh.

"Well my agent told me this act's a real sleeper —everyone who sees it goes to sleep. So—goodbye, kids!"

She fled the stage and would not look at Tom as she passed him.

Si was waiting, patient as always. Si the agent, coach, teacher, father, mother too after Mama's death. "You missed by just this much." He held his fingers several inches apart.

"Try that much, Pop," Laurie answered, pushing his hands until they were more like two feet apart. "Si, I think this is a big mistake."

"It's coming along, Laurie," he said. He gazed

at her fondly, holding her hands, sincere behind his tortoise shell glasses and his bulbous nose. Trying to smile away her worry.

"But these kids are too young for the material!"

There was a knock at the door and Tom came into the dressing room. He looked grave.

"It's coming along, eh Tom?" Si said.

"Well, it needs work." That wasn't what he really meant.

"Don't worry about it, Tom, we'll get it."

"I hope so." Tom shrugged. He had wanted to talk to Laurie alone but her father was never far from her side. He wondered how she managed to have anything to do with men. He was trying to figure out what to say next when someone outside paged him.

"He loves it!" Si said after Tom had gone.

Why does he always delude himself about me, Laurie thought. She yanked the ribbons out of her hair. And Si's old routines from the borscht circuit just didn't work on little kids in the seventies. Why wouldn't he see that? "Pop, Tom's a friend of yours," she said, "otherwise he would can me immediately."

"His being my friend has nothing to do with it." As always Si refused to believe what he saw.

"Pop," Laurie said patiently, "I appreciate your recommending me to Tom, but I really don't like the idea of replacing anybody to begin with—"

"Aw, come on—"

"No, Carolyn was *funny,* and I'm not. I just don't seem to get these kids at all . . ."

"You're doing fine," Si said. "Carolyn's leaving the show was a great break for you. Just work on your timing, honey. You know, timing is everything . . ."

Timing—that was his old story. Laurie looked at the clock. "Listen, Pop, I've got to go, I've booked a session for later this afternoon. Talk to you later, okay?"

"Okay. Remember—timing!"

Dear Si. I love you but don't tell me any more about timing or I'll scream.

Tom caught her at the outside door of the studio. "Laurie, wait a minute. I want to talk to you."

"Can't it wait? I'm running late." Laurie squirmed away from him and started toward the elevators.

"It's important." He clamped a meaty hand on her shoulder and held it there as she stood leaning on the down button.

"Listen, I don't want to depress you," he said in a low voice, "but there's talk about this show going network."

Laurie frowned, watching lights flash over the elevator. Eighteen, seventeen, sixteen . . . "Why should that depress me?"

"Well—they're talking about cutting you."

"Really?" Laurie was pleased and not pleased, since Kiddie Komedy had paid for this afternoon's recording session.

"I just wanted to tell you so that maybe you could get your act together," Tom said confiden-

24

tially. "You know, we had to use canned laughter today."

"Oh wow." That was a blow. She had never bombed *that* badly before. Laurie slumped under the weight of her bag.

"Hey look," Tom said eagerly. "I have some ideas that might make the act really work for those kids. Why don't you come by the office and we'll pitch 'em around a little?"

"But I'm really late now, I—" Fourteen, thirteen . . . The elevator was one floor away.

"What about tonight?"

Laurie stared at him. "I—uh—have plans already . . . " Didn't he know about Kenny? No, she supposed no one knew. She hardly ever talked about him. Kenny was her secret, regular life.

"Well, no harm in asking, is there?" Tom leered at her.

"Oh thanks anyway," Laurie said. When the elevator arrived she almost threw herself into it.

4.

The recording studio was at the other end of town. Laurie threw her bag onto the seat and eased the little red car into the steady flow of afternoon traffic. It was the time of day she usually had to herself and she regretted having to dash to the studio when she wanted nothing more than to be home at the piano. The thought of home brought a wry grin to her face: home *was* the piano—a baby grand took up a lot of space in a one-room apartment. Yet it was she who had insisted on getting the grand instead of a spinet that would certainly have fit better, because she insisted she needed the sound. She giggled, remembering the moving men. They had delivered the piano in several pieces and then stood shaking their heads trying to figure out just how to assemble it in a room only slightly larger than the instrument itself.

But Laurie didn't care that she had to sleep under a baby grand. "Hey, do you have a piano? Hey, do you have a piano?" she sang out the window, into the slowly moving traffic. "Hey, do you have a piano? Then you can write yourself a song about love." Words and music by Laurie Robinson, written at 3 A.M. the night of the piano's arrival, to celebrate same. They were going to record it now. She wondered if Richard and Ward, her backup singers, had had time to rehearse.

The traffic stopped, snarled up ahead by some construction on the road. "Hey, do you have a piano, then you can write yourself a song . . . about love." Laurie sighed out the last. Love. She wondered where the piano would end up after they were married. For the time being it was decided that Laurie would keep her apartment for a studio. But suppose she woke in the night, as she sometimes did, or or in the morning (like today), with a song in her head that couldn't wait? Would she get out of bed and *drive* to her piano? How would Kenny feel if she slept with the piano some nights instead of him? (She hadn't dared mention this up to now, knowing that such an idea would really upset him.) And yet Kenny was really more concerned about tennis than sex, she thought. Sometimes she suspected he *liked* playing tennis better.

She gazed absently at the line of cars, halted now, so close they appeared linked like a train. She remembered standing at the Spring Valley train station with Si and Mama, just before she died. And then without wanting to Laurie saw again the lobby of the Catholic hospital in Poughkeepsie, and the nun who had cared for her while Si went to make the arrangements for Mama's burial. The nun who had patiently explained, with a childlike insistence, how Mama wasn't dead but had gone to some palace of a place called Heaven. And she, Laurie, sophisticated child comedienne of twelve, had wanted so much to believe. But then there had been the coffin, the autumn smell of the graveyard she and Si had never visited again. "Your mama was a trooper, Laurie," Si had said, "She'd say 'the show must go on.' "

And it had gone on, Laurie thought, endlessly, it seemed to her then. After Mama's death, which coincided with her own adolescence, she became moody and restless. Always irritable. Unwilling. In trouble when she could be and off with her guitar the rest of the time. Even neglecting old Manny, her music teacher and friend. Until finally friends had suggested to Si that he move out West, break into TV and stay still for a while, so that Laurie could have some decent schooling. She chuckled at the memory of Si in the halls of Hollywood High, looking at the pictures of former students who were stars and picturing Laurie among them.

Faithful Si, her biggest fan, always promoting the act and the timing, and ignoring her music. At first he was ridiculously jealous of Manny, then the excuse was that he didn't like what she sang, it sounded too hillbilly. But that was because of Rick, the young American-hero-folksinger with the long hair who had taught her the guitar and seduced her behind the laundry shed at Minsingers when she was only thirteen. Yet long after Rick Tramper had gone off to a commune with Saritha the astrologer-waitress, after they had moved to Hollywood, Si's attitude toward her music had persisted. It was his competition, he felt (though he never said it). He was afraid she really loved music more than she loved him. So he never paid it much attention, or pretended that part of her life didn't exist.

And after Laurie had moved into her tiny apartment and was attending junior college, she had stopped inviting him to the little off-campus clubs where she and the guys, and later Annie and Bonnie, performed. Because Si never came. Kenny came sometimes, but although he liked to hear her sing he wasn't really interested in her success as a singer. It freaked her a little that both Si and Kenny, the two people who loved her the most, didn't care about her music. But somehow that didn't deter her.

Although they do wear me down, she thought suddenly, and then wondered, as she had been doing all week, whether she really did love Kenny. And what she was doing anyway, proposing to spend the rest of her life in this Hollywood she had never identified with, although paradoxically it was the only real *home* she'd known.

She swung into the vast asphalt expanse of the

parking lot, half-empty now at four thirty in the afternoon. The late sun shone white on the studio windows. She felt better knowing only music lay ahead, at least for the moment, and as she swung through the revolving door into the air-conditioned lobby, she was singing:

It's a long way from Brooklyn to L.A.
Sometimes I wonder why I came here anyway
But I've got the songs I write and sing
And the sunshine promises that Hollywood
   can bring.*

* Copyright © 1977 by Big Hill Music Company

5.

The elevator opened into a large reception area where seated people were staring at the floor or at the receptionist, who was gazing into space with her ear to the phone. Laurie went straight to the desk without looking at anyone because she was almost a half-hour late, and she wasn't sure whether by this time she'd missed the space. She wondered if Richard and Ward had signed her in. "Hi, I'm Laurie Robinson—"

"Excuse me a minute." The receptionist turned away.

Laurie swung around to hide her annoyance and looked straight at the Richard and Ward she'd been thinking about, whose harmony was perfect but whose appearances clashed: Richard was tall, dark, poetic, intense; Ward looked more like a gnome. They were sprawled all over a fancy

velveteen couch, leering at her horribly. At the moment neither had his shoes on.

"Oh, *there* you are," Laurie said, feeling stupid and awfully glad to see them. They too hired out for commercials by day and played their own music at night. They knew the conflicts. She flopped down on the couch between them, grateful for the near bodies of sympathetic friends. "Did you have time to rehearse?"

"Uh—no," Richard confessed. "But I got this—look!" From a manila envelope he carefully extracted an eight-by-ten glossy portfolio shot of himself in which he looked unusually handsome.

"You'll need more than that, gorgeous!" Laurie teased. "Next time you'd better rehearse!"

Just then the elevator doors opened and Annie Gerrard stumbled in, her curly blond hair even wilder than usual and a desperate expression on her normally cheerful face. She was waving a script and muttering. Ward jumped up to make room for her.

"You're even later than me—what's the matter?" Laurie asked.

Annie slumped into the soft couch, staring into space. "The commercial I just auditioned for—it was a circus," she said.

Laurie nodded sympathetically.

"But I had a callback at Wakeford."

"You mean Fenwick Farms?"

"Can you believe it?" Annie laughed. "How'd Kiddie Komedy go?" She patted Laurie's hand maternally. Annie mothered everyone.

"It sucked," Laurie said after a minute.

"That bad?" Annie's wide blue eyes got wider.

"Annie, I think they're gonna give me the axe." Laurie was surprised at how easy it was to say that. She really didn't care, even if it upset Si.

"Why don't you just tell Si you don't want to do it?"

"I've told him, Annie. Over and over again: 'I'm not a commedienne, I just want to sing my songs and act.' But it's like he doesn't hear me. Well, maybe this will convince him," she added thoughtfully. "Getting dropped could be a blessing in disguise."

"Oh come on, Laurie, it's not that bad. I saw the show last week and it made *me* laugh."

"You and my father and no one else," Laurie said. "They even had to use canned laughter today. I'm just not *funny*, Annie . . ."

"Oh stop it, you're a genius."

"Yeah? Tell that to the Fenwick director."

Richard announced from the doorway that the studio would be free in three minutes. Laurie stood up, helped Annie to struggle out of the plushy couch. "I wanted to talk," she said to Annie, "but I guess there's no time."

"Have dinner with me," Annie said. "Jerry's out of town."

"I can't I've got to practice . . ."

"You gotta have *dinner*." Annie's blue eyes flashed worry. "You haven't been eating, right? I can tell."

"Oh, Annie . . ."

"You can go home right after." Annie had put her foot down. Annie was insisting.

"Okay, Earth Mother." Laurie smiled. No matter how it arrived, she was always grateful for Annie's concern. "Where?"

"Casey's," Annie said promptly. "My sister Gail's coming."

The doors in front of them opened silently.

"Laurie, we're on," Richard whispered.

It took them until eight o'clock, but the tape sounded pretty good, Laurie thought. She wondered what everyone else was thinking.

"Sounded good in the phones," Annie said. "How'd it feel?"

"Felt good," Ward declared.

"Yeah, we had a good groove going." Richard sometimes talked cool. "Think we should do this *professionally*?" he said, this time like a hick.

They all laughed as they headed for the control booth, hoping. Only the playback would tell.

6.

Casey's was a fashionable bar where film and TV people gathered to see each other and to be seen, they hoped, by the ones who did the hiring. There were lots of nooks and crannies, dark spaces for intrigue, and old pictures of Humphrey Bogart on the walls. It was hard to tell employees from customers, since most of the people who worked there had the same ambitions.

Laurie, who only wanted a quiet booth in the back, found Annie waiting at a table right in the middle, which was just like her: Annie liked being in the center of things. "Well, here we are in the heart of Hollywood!" she said loudly. "Two young actresses heading straight for the top!"

Several people nearby grinned at her. That kind of bravado at least got attention.

Normally Laurie loved Annie's chatter and un-

selfconscious good humor; Annie could laugh anyone out of the blues. But now Laurie hid behind
the menu until she stopped clowning.

"What's the matter, kid?" Annie asked.

"I need to get out of this business."

"Me too." Annie shook her curls and batted her
long lashes. "But what could we do instead?"

"I don't know." Gloomy, Laurie laughed in spite
of herself. "But anything would be better than
what I had to do today."

"Hey—want to learn how to draw?" Annie
waved a matchbook in the air. "It says right here
we could be artists in fourteen hours." She
grinned. "We could leave for Paris tomorrow . . . "

"And get a studio . . . " Laurie imagined the
baby grand in a *real* studio.

"With lots of paints and easels . . . "

"And my piano . . . "

" . . . and lots of naked men lying around,"
Annie added, "just for the effect."

"And no more commercials." Laurie grimaced.
"Annie, those people are making me crazy. I can't
seem to do their stuff."

"Oh, I forgot to tell you," Annie said. "I got that
Fenwick Farms commercial."

"The one with the eggs?"

"Yeah." Annie looked at her. "What's the matter—you mad at me?"

"Of course not. In fact I'm glad you got it—I
know you need the money. But—how did you
understand that director?"

"Oh, I didn't understand him," Annie said. "I

never understand any of those guys. He just kept telling me to do things his way and I kept doing them my way, and finally he said I was great, gave me his watch, and hired me."

Laurie burst out laughing. *Annie and her priceless self-confidence*, she thought. "Just tell me, how'd you say that one line, what was it—oh, 'No *wonder* you're having trouble making fluffy omelets . . .'"

Annie sat back and chewed her lip. "Hmm, let's see. I think I said it something like this." She cleared her throat and recited, in almost a monotone: "No wonder you're having trouble making fluffy omelets."

"You said it like that?" Laurie asked, amazed. That wasn't anywhere near what the director had said he wanted. "I don't know why I bother to listen to these shmucks," she said, shaking her head.

"Oh, you should *never* listen to them," Annie assured her. "I always just keep doing it the way I want to do it. Sooner or later they think I'm doing it their way."

Laurie smiled. She wished she had Annie's patience and natural humor. Annie would probably walk away with the Kiddie Komedy Hour if she had the chance.

The waitress arrived and took their orders; she was someone they'd gone to school with. "Wanna go to Paris?" Annie joked, straight-faced, holding up the matchbook.

"Yes, we're leaving tomorrow," Laurie said, picking up the line. "We're gonna be artists."

"And there'll be lots of naked men lying around . . . "

"Save me a seat," the waitress said as she left.

They collapsed, laughing. "Oh I'm too hungry to laugh," Annie protested, clutching her stomach. "Since Jerry's been gone I've been starving myself, it's a good excuse to diet."

"How long's he going to be away?"

"Only a couple more days."

"So he'll be back for the wedding?" It was the first time all day Laurie had said the word out loud. It terrified her. Her heart began thundering.

"Don't worry, Laurie, I wouldn't let my old man miss your wedding," Annie paused, noting Laurie's expression. "What's the matter, hon?"

"Oh, I don't know, Annie." Suddenly she didn't feel like talking about Ken and Si and all her doubts and fears in the middle of Casey's. And they seemed so unfounded. But the work problem was real too. "Well I don't know what to do about the act," she said.

"Is that all? You know what you need? You need a new angle." Annie launched into her opinion enthusiastically. "You gotta loosen up a little." She sat back in lip-chewing position and thought a minute. "Hey—I got an idea. Hand me Larry, I got a bit for you . . . "

"Annie, please not here."

"Aw, come on, sour face," Annie begged. "It'll only take a minute."

With a sigh Laurie reached into her bag and handed her the dummy.

"Now suppose Larry were my grandmother—it'd be perfect," Annie began, propping Larry on her lap.

"Annie, please—I've had a rough day," Laurie said. She was beginning to feel dizzy and everyone was of course looking at them, expecting a performance. And with Larry—

"Hello, Frances? This is Sadie," Annie went on.

Laurie couldn't stand it. She knew Annie was only trying to make her feel better. But the game wasn't working. "I gotta call my answering service," she said, grabbing her wallet out of her bag. She stood up and, fighting tears, went toward the back where the phone was.

7.

There was someone on the phone. Laurie stood blinking into her wallet, fishing for change. She got out a dime finally, closed the wallet, and leaned against the wall, trying to calm down. At least it was quiet back here. She was standing in a hallway that led to the rest rooms, just outside a narrow alcove where the phone was.

The young man talking had his back to her. He was wearing a brown shirt of lightweight cotton that fit him well and she remarked the ease of his posture. Laurie always noticed men. Admiring his back gave her mind a rest anyway. But then she automatically compared it with Kenny's. Thinking of Kenny wasn't too hard but she was tormented by the way she had reacted to the word wedding. Where had this terrible fear come from? She was sure she hadn't felt that way a couple of weeks ago. It was weird, she thought, turning her gaze from the young man to a blonde woman passing by in a hurry, whom she recognized as Carla Wright, a popular young actress. Passing Laurie with a silent nod, Carla tapped the young man on the shoulder and smiled as he turned around. Still talking he nodded absently at her.

Laurie watched Carla disappear without interest; she had worked with Carla, who was a good actress but a bitch to be around (all the men were always hers). Not that Laurie had ever cared a lot; because the Hollywood types she met didn't usually attract her. Anyway, there had always been Kenny, the boy of her dreams, a regular kid from a regular family whose father wasn't in show business, and who offered her steady love, a home, real life. She wondered if he'd called her. She felt terribly guilty about her fear of the wedding because Kenny wanted it so much. But she knew she'd feel better if she could just talk to him. She decided to call the answering service first and then if he hadn't called to call his house.

If this *guy* would ever get off the phone. Laurie looked to find him staring at her, as though he were far more interested in her than his own conversation. He had dark curly hair like Kenny's but the face was older, the brown eyes knowing and direct. Laurie felt herself challenged. She stared back at him.

"I understand, don't worry, it'll work out fine, Roy's finishing the charts now," he said. "Have you heard from Jerry?" Still looking at Laurie he waved his finger from her to the phone. "I'll just be a minute," he said to her.

Laurie nodded.

"Yes, but what about Jerry," he said into the phone.

She looked away but found herself very aware of his presence nonetheless, and glancing at him, noted the outline of his body under the thin cotton, the worry line that divided his forehead in two. She stood outside the alcove all the while he spoke to Mark about Jerry, aware that he was also looking at her from time to time and caught in the game of it.

When he finally hung up she risked a look at him again. He smiled, the question still in his eyes, and stepped out of the alcove. "It's all yours," he said. He seemed to want to say something else because he hesitated before he went past her along the hall without speaking.

But he had gone only a few steps when he stopped and turned, said "Oh shit!" and coming back grabbed the phone out of Laurie's hand. She had just begun to dial the answering service. He clicked the receiver arm until her dime fell through and then immediately put his dime in and began dialing. "Listen, excuse me, I gotta make this one fast call, really it's urgent," he said. "Here's your dime."

"My god," Laurie protested, "you're certainly number one, aren't you." With a disgusted look she took the dime and started down the hall.

There was a detaining hand on her arm suddenly. "Dont go away. Please. Please not yet. Please."

She turned. He was joking but his eyes were very soft. "Really, I'll only be a minute," he said. "I'm sorry."

Laurie felt as if nothing could keep her from falling into those eyes. But this was a ridiculous scene. "Look, my dinner's getting cold," she lied (she had ordered a tunafish salad).

He shook his head and putting an arm around her, pulled her into the alcove. "You can't go now," he whispered. "This is a very important call and you're a very important part of it."

Laurie tried to shrink inside her flesh within the circle of his arm but they were too crowded together in the little alcove. Of course she could have elbowed her way out at any time but she was so astonished at his ease that without protest she allowed it to be what it was: an embrace of sorts. He smelled nice and his lips were dark and full.

"Operator," he said, "I want to call person-to-person collect to New York, the number is 212 759-8720, and I want to speak to Mr. Jerome Bennett. My name is Chris Nolan . . ."

"And what's your name?"

"Laurie."

". . . and Laurie," he said into the phone, squeezing her shoulder.

She really didn't like being used as a prop for a phone call, and the squeeze prompted her to decide that she really ought to put a stop to this situation before the whole thing got out of hand. "Listen, I'm hungry," she began, struggling a little. "I hardly ate all day, and . . ."

"Shh, we're waiting on destiny here." He grinned at her.

She stopped struggling. Destiny? He was outrageous!

"Hello, Jerry? Listen, I just spoke to Mark—how close are we to a deal? How much? Take it! No, I'm serious, tell Mark I spoke to you . . . Terrific—yes, you've made me a very happy man, and Laurie is a very happy woman . . . right! Goodbye!"

She managed to extricate herself when he hung up. "Congratulate me!" he said, beaming.

"Congratulations," Laurie said wryly, extending her hand.

But that look returned to his eyes, and as he took her hand instead of shaking it he pulled her to him and kissed her. It was dynamite. Laurie's knees went weak, without thinking she kissed him back.

"That was a terrific kiss! That was a terrific kiss!" he shouted into the hallway.

Laurie stepped back, shocked, less amazed at him than at herself. He grabbed her hand. "Can I buy you a drink?"

"I have to make a phone call."

"I'll wait."

"—and I have dinner and my friends waiting for me . . ."

"And now you have *me* waiting too." He leaned

against the wall and when Laurie frowned he merely smiled, perfectly at ease.

She dialed the service with a slightly shaking hand. There weren't any messages. She held the receiver to her ear for a while after the phone clicked off, trying to decide whether to call Kenny. But she didn't want to call him while this *person* was watching her and worse, while she felt herself caught in something unaccountably strong, a feeling one either obeyed or struggled hard to overcome. She put the receiver back on its hook and turned to him.

"Any calls?" he said.

"No."

"Were you expecting one?"

"Uh . . . no." Something kept her from saying she had expected Kenny. She knew she ought to but she couldn't.

"Good, then listen, I have a confession to make," he said.

"What kind of confession?" What was he talking about?

"My confession is that I really don't want to buy you a drink." He said this rather sorrowfully.

"Well, that's okay." Feeling unexpectedly disappointed, Laurie started past him.

"What I really want—" He seized her waist as she walked around him. "What I *really* want is to take you home with me."

My god, he certainly was up front about it! Laurie pulled away, shaking her head but grinning at him anyway because she was pleased with the flattery. "Well, but I can't—" She fished for an excuse. "You see I'm with friends . . ."

"Can't I be your friend?"

"Sure, but I can't go with you, really . . ." For some reason she couldn't bring herself to say "because I'm getting married on Sunday." She looked at him, trying to find in his eyes some friendly acquiescence.

But he wouldn't accept her refusal. He looked at her for a moment and then, pulling her with him into the alcove, kissed her again in a way that made clear he was dead serious. Then he let go of her. "I'll be at the bar," he said, "and I'll be waiting there forever for you."

"I . . . can't." Refusing again Laurie realized how very much she wanted to say yes. "I really can't," she repeated, as though to convince herself.

"Oh yes you can." He spoke very softly, then turned on his heel and almost immediately was gone from the hall.

8.

Annie's sister Gail had arrived. When Laurie got back to the table Annie was in mid-description of the dress she had bought for Laurie's wedding. "Gail," she said dramatically, "it's the most beautiful dress you've ever seen, it's a gorgeous peach color, you would *die* to wear it . . ."

Gail, who was into tee shirts, scowled.

"Well, maybe *you* wouldn't die to wear it," Annie said, a little miffed, "but somebody would. It's got embroidery on the shoulders and all down the arms . . ."

Gail was rifling through her pocketbook. "Those bastards from the IRS are auditing me again," she grumbled.

"Gail, I was talking about a *dress* . . ."

"I know, I know," Gail replied irritably. "But they're after *me!*" She turned to Laurie, who was just sitting down. "Why *me?*"

"What? What'd you say, Gail?" Laurie felt confused enough without having to answer questions.

"We were just talking about a dress and got off the subject," Annie said sarcastically.

Laurie looked at them, trying to project herself into the immediate present and forget what had just happened. The tuna salad sat in front of her but although before she had been starving she was no longer even remotely interested. It might as well have been a cut-paper arrangement, or a pile of stones. Her heart had begun beating rapidly again and she could feel the sweat gathering at her temples. She looked toward the bar but didn't see him.

There was a hand on her shoulder and she jumped. A fork clattered to the floor. Laurie looked up to see Carla Wright, who was just squeezing through a narrow space between their table and the next.

"How're you doing?" Carla had always felt friendly toward Laurie, who had never tried to compete with her.

"Uh—okay," Laurie said, struggling to believe it. There was a short, awkward silence during which she became aware that Annie and Gail had stopped talking and were staring at Carla. She introduced them. Carla said hello and then left.

"So that's Carla Wright," Annie said. "Well I don't like her."

"But you just met her . . ."

"I've also *heard* a lot about her."

"I heard she's up for the lead in *Pumpkin Face*," Gail said.

"No, I heard they're still looking." Laurie was glad to have something to talk about. "Jesse tried to get me an audition but he said they weren't seeing very many girls." She looked at the bar again. There he was.

"Carla'll probably get it, she's hot right now." This from Gail, said with authority.

"You never can tell," Annie cautioned. Though she loved Gail she made it a point never to agree with her if she could help it. "They want someone who can sing too. They don't want to have to dub it . . ."

"Well I think they'll use Carla and they'll *have* to dub it," Gail argued.

"Can't she sing?" Laurie had been listening with one ear. The other was attending the confusion inside her, the pull of these strange and painful waves of desire that kept up despite any other distractions.

"Carla can't *sing*," Annie said with her mouth full. "I don't even thing she can *act*." She chewed hard and deliberately on a piece of French bread.

"Oh no, she's a good actress," Laurie said vaguely. What did she care? She picked up her fork and made a half-hearted stab at the tunafish, then looked back to the bar again. He was talking to another guy. He was gesturing. She remembered his hand on the phone, long slender dark fingers.

"I *hate* Carla Wright," Annie said miserably. Annie was like that sometimes.

Laurie sighed. "Look, Annie, there's room in this town for all of us, right?"

"Yeah, I guess I was a little harsh." She leaned across the table and leered at Laurie. With her distorted mouth and curly hair she looked like a pretty little troll. "Let's wait for her in the alley and beat the shit outta her," she hissed.

Laurie grinned and reached out to tweak Annie's nose, the way Si had always teased her when she behaved like a smart-ass. Then, like someone dreaming, her subconscious having come to a decision independently and without her knowledge, she transferred her napkin from her lap to the table, got out her wallet and slowly zipped up the bag where Larry the Dummy lay on his back, staring (accusing?). Then she stood up suddenly, almost knocking over her chair. "Well, I've got to go," she mumbled. "Goodnight everyone."

"What—where're you going?" Annie stared at her. "You haven't eaten!"

"Uh, something's come up."

"Laurie, what the hell's wrong?" Annie said in her serious voice, which never rose above a whisper.

"Listen, Annie, do me a favor, okay?" With her eyes Laurie begged not to be questioned further. She counted out some bills from her wallet. "If this isn't enough to cover my check will you let me know tomorrow?"

"Where are you going?" Now Annie was all Earth Mother and no joke.

"Trust me," Laurie said, smiling.

"Why should I?"

"I don't know." She didn't even trust herself. Annie's worried expression hovered. "You didn't even *touch* your food," she said. "Are you sure you're all right? You look pale!"

"I'm fine, I'm fine . . ." Laurie mumbled. "Goodnight, Gail, good to see you again."

"You hardly saw me," Gail said.

"Oh, well I'm sorry, I'll see you again soon. Tomorrow Annie, okay?"

She walked away. Annie watched her go, resisting an urge to get up and follow her. It wasn't like Laurie to just go off like that. "It must be pre-wedding jitters," she told Gail. But she had a funny feeling it was something more.

"Excuse me, excuse me." Laurie threaded her way among the tables, with difficulty because of the bag that kept threatening to sweep away people's plates. He was still sitting at the bar talking to that guy. When she was almost there he seemed familiar in some sense, but unreal. She wanted to touch him, to verify him. She approached from behind and tapped him on the shoulder.

When Chris turned around and saw her his mouth literally dropped open. He hadn't expected her. He thought his whole act had failed despite her response to his kiss and the tension that had filled the phone alcove.

51

"I accept," Laurie said, looking right at him.

His eyes widened with pleasure at the simplicity of her statement. He climbed down from the bar-stool and put an arm gently, casually around her shoulder, as though some compact had been concluded. "What about your friends?" he teased.

"I told them that destiny called," Laurie grinned.

"Well okay then, you are *on*," he said, but very quietly and seriously, not like the shout in the hall. He downed his drink and reached for her bag. "Do you always carry your overnight case?" he said when he felt the weight of it.

"No, it's—" How to say there was a dummy inside?

"Its okay," Chris said. "Don't explain." He turned to his friend. "Goodnight, Charley," he said, rather pointedly Laurie thought.

"What?" Charley looked puzzled.

"I said 'goodnight, Charley,'" Chris replied, with a broad grin and a glance at Laurie.

It was the kind of macho exchange she usually deplored but all Laurie wanted now was to get out of Casey's so she overlooked it. They started away from the bar.

"Wait—" Charley called. "How're you getting home?"

Chris looked at Laurie. "Do you have a car?"

"Yes."

"I have a ride." With a nod to the still confused Charley he closed his hand firmly around Laurie's arm and steered her toward the door.

9.

Earlier there had been a brief but heavy rain and now the street outside Casey's was dark and glistening. Because Laurie was wearing open shoes they had to jump over puddles, which eased the tension between them somewhat, and gave her a reason to be holding lightly to those long fingers. By the time they got to the car she felt she knew him better. Although she did not know him, there was no justification she could invent for what she was doing. No rationalization possible at all.

It wasn't even the wedding fear, she thought, after they were in the car, although she realized it was probably that somewhere in her head. But mainly she felt this adventure was about him, this Chris Nolan. And now it was about the clear night too, and the road. Following his directions, she headed west, toward the ocean. There wasn't much traffic.

As though by agreement neither asked for specifics of the other's personal life. Their work was enough of a basis for conversation; he was a director, she an actress. They spoke of Hollywood—he was from New York but working out West now. They told stories of coping with the madness of it. Laurie described Fenwick Farms; he was sympathetic, he hated stupidity, over-analysis.

There was a long light at Santa Monica Boulevard. Laurie glanced at him. God, he was attractive. "Were you really giong to wait forever?" she asked lightly.

"At least all night." He was serious.

"I couldn't let you do that." *What a line,* she thought. And this driving to a rendezvous with a stranger was a play, or a movie maybe. Yes, it was a movie. *About destiny,* she thought, and she felt scared to death. What if it turned out to be true? No, this was *not* the life she was going to live. *And yet its me,* Laurie told herself, *this is me doing this now.* She felt panicky and drove faster, but kept neat control of the little red car, which knowing so well she could always handle. It crossed her mind that she wouldn't ever be able to sell it, now that it was taking her through this night.

"You're a good driver," he said, leaning back against the seat and stretching his legs. He put his arm across the top of the seat and held her shoulder lightly, just to reestablish some physical contact between them because he had felt her withdraw.

"Do you live near the beach?" Laurie asked. They were only a few blocks away; she could hear the ocean.

"I live right smack on it," he said, then smiled at her evident pleasure, the hair that fell over her cheek. He brushed it back. "You'll see," he whispered. "You'll like it."

He was right. It seemed as if the whole back wall of the apartment was glass; beyond it the dark Pacific churned at the foot of a rocky slope. It wasn't really his since it belonged to a friend currently occupying his New York apartment, but he liked to think of it as home. They toured; in each room stopped to kiss, to fondle, to breathe, swallow, wait, hold it back. Over drinks Chris confided he's always thought a home important because he hadn't had much of one as a kid. Laurie understood that. He'd been hustling a long time, he said. Watching his easy grace as he mixed drinks and pulled curtains and lowered lights (the living room had a built-in dimmer), Laurie couldn't imagine him ever having been deprived; he seemed more a well-loved, confident, sophisticated man who'd been adored all his life. He grinned at her observation: by one's thirties, he countered (wisely and very seductively), one has to let the past just ride, and to "seize the time," he said, live in the present. "Like you and me," he said. "You and me and a telephone."

He was sitting facing her on a long-cream-colored couch when he said that. Remembering the first pressure of his body against her in the phone alcove Laurie opened her arms to him now in frank admission of desire, her characteristic reticence gone as she smoothed her hands over the warm soft cotton back, pressed him to her.

"You know, you're very pretty," he said, teasing, as though he had just discovered that.

"Oh I am not," Laurie said modestly. "Besides comediennes are not supposed to be."

"Well you are." He sat up, pulling her with him, and kissed her. "Yes, you are pretty."

"You don't have to flatter me, you know," Laurie said as they stood up. "I'll sleep with you anyway."

With a little laugh he grabbed her, put one arm around her and began to unbutton her blouse. "Then let's find the bed quick," he said. "I didn't think you came just to see my house."

He knows it all, Laurie thought later. *Everything a man should know about making love.* She felt very sleepy, not tired, but afloat in her own drowsy body. She touched him. "Chris," she said.

"What?"

"Nothing. I just wanted to say your name."

"God I'm tired," he murmured. "Got to take a vacation one of these years . . ."

Laurie shifted slightly to look at him. His eyes were closed. "Sleep well, Chris," she said. "Sleep well."

10.

Laurie woke slowly and rolled over in the wide bed, blinking at the sight of unfamiliar curtains and missing the dark wooden length of the piano beside her. She sat up.

Chris was gone. Their clothes lay scattered on the white shag rug like a photo-montage, the most intimate apparel on top. Laurie grabbed her underwear off the pile but then decided to wait to dress until after she'd showered. Not seeing anything like a robe immediately available she slipped on his shirt, the thin brown cotton that smelled of him. It made her shiver and think of pleasure. But the daylight at the end of the curtains warned her off. Pulling them open she remembered, as the unbuttoned shirt fell open and bright sun warmed her naked body, that today was Wednesday. The wedding rehearsal was on

Wednesday, and after it dinner with Kenny and his parents. *Oh god, I've got to get out of here,* she thought suddenly.

After a search she found Chris in the kitchen making breakfast. With a plateful of eggs in his hand he turned to her, cheerful and self-possessed. She wished she felt the same. "Oh there you are," she said.

"Good morning," he said, bowing.

"I didn't know where you were," Laurie mumbled. She felt awkward as hell.

"Well here I am," he said, and with a smile turned back to the stove. "Did you sleep well?"

"Yes. How long have you been up?"

"Oh, hours."

She thought of him watching her asleep and felt vulnerable.

"Uh, I'm wearing your shirt," she said. "I hope that's okay."

"It's terrific," he said. "But let me get you a clean one."

"Oh no." She backed off, afraid he'd touch her and she wouldn't be able to leave. "This one's fine, I was just about to take a shower anyway . . ."

"Not before breakfast," he said. "It's almost ready. Here's your juice."

"Oh . . . thank you." She wasn't used to being waited on by men. Usually she waited on Si, also on Kenny a bit. A bit too much, she always thought.

"You're welcome." She looked so damn young standing there he felt strange.

Laurie sipped the juice, which was delicious. "You make this?"

He nodded.

"Fresh-squeezed?"

"Yeah, we New Yorkers know how to do things right." He grinned and headed for the dining room.

The clock suddenly appeared in front of her nose although it had been there all the time. "God, I didn't realize it was nine o'clock," she gasped. "Here, let me give you a hand." She grabbed the eggs and a basket of toast and followed him.

An electric pot was waiting, its little red light on. "What do you take in your coffee?"

"Oh I don't drink it, the caffeine makes me crazy."

He hesitated, raised his eyebrows. "You want tea?"

"No no, that's got tannic acid."

"A glass of water?" he asked finally. She could see he didn't quite know what to do with her.

"Not unless you've got some vitamins," she said.

"No, I don't." He shrugged. "You take a lot of vitamins?"

"Yeah sure, they're good for you."

He was silent, eating.

"I'm a vitamin freak," Laurie went on. She felt herself gaining confidence from this difference. What could they ever mean to each other if he didn't take vitamins? "B-complex, iron, C's, and lots of E—but only at night, though."

"Only at night?"

"Well, you've got to take the E twelve hours after you take the iron, or else the iron cancels out the E . . ."

He stared at her. She was a little weird, he thought. But he found that attractive, more so than the usual pretty conformity starlets had to offer. It seemed there was something *to* her, though he didn't know what.

"Why are you looking at me that way?" Laurie demanded.

"Can't I look at you?" He reached across the table and put his hand inside the brown shirt, on her breast.

She pulled away, her nipple hard, a tightness in her throat. How was she going to tell him? Laurie swallowed. "What time is it?" she asked.

"Ten after nine."

"I'd better get going."

"Where are you going?"

"Oh, I have a really busy day today, uh—I've got a commercial audition in the morning and a rehearsal in the afternoon—"

"What kind of rehearsal?"

"A—wedding rehearsal," Laurie whispered.

"Oh? Whose wedding?"

"Mine."

He froze, the coffee cup hovered near his lips. "Yours?" He put the cup down.

"Uh-huh. Mine." She looked at him, half in

sorrow, half in fear. What the hell would he think of her? What could anyone think of her going off with a stranger five days before her wedding?

"You've got to be kidding, man," Chris said. He looked shocked.

"No." The lump in her throat was so large she was sure it was visible.

"When are you getting married?" he asked quietly.

"Sunday."

"*This* Sunday?"

"Yes." Laurie traced the napkin design with her fork.

"Uh, tell me . . . do you do this kind of thing often?" There was the anger, just below the surface of the remark.

"Oh, almost never," she assured him, anxious to protest her innocence. He was silent so she ventured: "Do you?"

"Now and then," he said wryly. But he still couldn't believe her. "Are you *really* getting married on Sunday?"

Laurie nodded, several times. The tears came to her eyes. She blinked.

"Okay," he said. "Okay."

"Are you . . . married?" Laurie asked, not that it mattered.

"Separated."

"Well, there you go." She didn't know what she meant by that and from his uncomfortable attitude she knew it was time to go. "I'd better take my shower now," she said, standing. "I've got a ten thirty call."

She fled then, leaving him bewildered at the table, but stopped on her way to the bathroom to look out the wide window that faced the beach. There were gulls and small birds feeding onshore and then beyond them the sea, constant, sparkling, calm. It was a beautiful scene and she was very keenly aware that she would probably never see it again. She went back into the dining room where he was still sitting, drinking his coffee and staring into space. "When you were married . . ." she began hesitantly.

"Yes?"

"Did you do this kind of thing anyway?"

"Only if I found a girl as beautiful as you," he said, only half joking.

Laurie went to him then, kissed him, cradled his head on her breast. "You know you make breakfast better than you tell stories," she said. Then she went to get dressed.

Half an hour later they walked in silence toward the little red car, which though jaunty looked like a poor relation come to visit. Self-consciously Laurie smoothed a piece of the adhesive tape that was coming loose from the canvas top. Chris stowed her bag in the back seat, closed the door for her and then leaned against the car as (with some effort and careful listening) she started it.

Now all I have to do is go, Laurie thought, but that was easier said than done. She looked up at him. He seemed lost in thought. Then suddenly he stuck his head in the window, his face close to hers.

"Let me ask you something," he said in a rush. "What was this—some sort of a last fling before you got married?"

Laurie shook her head. "Last fling . . ." *No no —it was just that I wanted you, it was—* She couldn't finish the thought. "I really don't know why it happened, you know?" she said, her voice wavering a little. "It just . . . happened." She cleared her throat.

He traced the curve of her cheek with his finger. "Well, I'm glad it happened," he said. "I liked it. You don't have to apologize."

"I know." Laurie sighed. "I liked it too. But well, its just that my fiancé was working . . ." That was probably a lie. "I don't want to talk about it," she said finally.

Her attitude did not go unnoticed. "How long have you been engaged?" he asked, thinking her too young to have made such a decision.

"Six months."

"Do you live with him?"

"No."

"Why not?" He seemed surprised.

"We—just don't," Laurie said. Kenny lived at home, with his parents, where he had always lived. She stuck out her lip as though she had been insulted or accused of something backward or unsophisticated.

"Have you known him long?"

64

"Since high school." Laurie ventured a look at him. "Why are you asking me all these questions?"

"It gets me hot," he said pointedly, almost derisively. It was the defensive position of a man altogether unused to losing.

Laurie ignored that. "I'd better go," she said. He pulled his head out of the car, straightened up, then just stood there with the sun making red highlights in his dark hair and those long fingers hooked in his belt loops. She wanted to say goodbye nicely. "Thanks for breakfast," she said.

"You're very welcome."

"I'm sorry," she said at last, meaning it so much.

He came back to the car and planted his mouth on hers, his tongue parting their lips. Laurie let go of the wheel to clasp his neck.

"You want to come back later?" he murmured. "Tonight maybe?"

"Oh I can't, I really can't."

"Okay, goodbye then," he said, withdrawing once more.

"Goodbye," Laurie whispered. She released the emergency, put the car in gear, and started slowly away.

"Hey Laurie? Wait a minute!"

Frightened, she jammed on the brake.

"I don't even know your last name—to call you or anything . . ."

"That's okay, really," she said, swallowing hard.

She was trembling. Why wouldn't he just let her *go*?

He raised his hands in a gesture of exasperation. "Have a nice day," he said, sullenly she thought.

Laurie stepped on the gas. At the end of the drive she looked in the rear-view mirror. He was still standing there watching the car, his hands hooked in his belt loops, shaking his head. She watched him get smaller and smaller as she drove away.

11.

The audition was in a large studio on North Radford Avenue. She got there early, having driven over the speed limit almost every mile of the way, while making a vain attempt not to think. The red car shuddered a little when she shut it off. She patted the dashboard like a concerned mother. The radio said it was ten fifteen. Laurie shut that off too and sat back and closed her eyes. She had parked under some trees, thinking it better to leave the car in the shade, but now she felt chilly. She rolled up the windows and then sat immobile once more, staring straight ahead at a picket fence that marked the perimeter of the lot. Nearby, against the side of a small brick garage, a torn poster flapped in the breeze. A black squirrel ran down the trunk of one tree and up the trunk of another. A horn sounded from the avenue. Everything seemed normal, yet Laurie felt as though she were going to die. She put her head down on the steering wheel and cried her heart out for a minute.

After that she felt better. But what seemed like a videotape of the whole insane adventure lay at the edge of her consciousness threatening to turn itself on. She glared at herself in the rear-view mirror and then got out of the car. As Si would inevitably say, the show must go on.

Both Annie and Bonnie were also up for the audition. By ten forty-five they were assembled: the director, Richmond, Max the producer, and the ever-present executive from the ad agency in his usual suit and tie. Plus assorted technicians. Laurie groaned when she saw the cameraman, who had a reputation for being difficult.

The subject was waffles, Mrs. Franklin's waffles. The client was hoping Mrs. Franklin would challenge the supremacy of Aunt Jemina. From the look of things, that didn't seem likely.

The three girls, each holding a box of waffles, were dressed in early American costumes identical to the one Mrs. Franklin wore on the box. They were standing (Laurie in the middle) in front of a scenery flat to which an enlarged photo of a cornfield had been stapled. In front of the flat an American flag waved on a pole. The flag was mounted with floor brackets that creaked a little every time the pole moved in the blast of air from the wind machine. The noise reminded Laurie of a closet door she used to creak on purpose to bug Si one summer when they were playing Grossingers. And the cool open studio with its shafts of sunlight at the second story might have been in the Catskills. She found herself thinking of the old wooden laundry building and of Rick Tramper (how she had *loved* him!). Or so she'd thought, then. Love. What the hell was it supposed to be? Really. She was trying to concentrate on being where she was but she kept thinking ahead to the wedding rehearsal and feelings of panic would seize her.

The assistant director was starting things up. "Quiet everybody . . . okay, let's roll."

The dust settled. Silence. "Speed," the mixer said after a moment.

"Mark it."

The cameraman's assistant stepped up importantly. He was eighteen and breaking in. "X58, take 41, Mrs. Franklin's Waffles," he said in a melodious voice. He clapped the slate and disappeared behind the lights.

"Okay action," Richmond called.

"Roast 'em! Toast 'em! Put 'em in your oven! Eat Mrs. Franklin's Waffles every morning!"

"Cut!"

Richmond walked up to them, a large florid man in a Hawaiian shirt with waves riding across its front pockets. Each time he took a breath it seemed the sea was moving. Laurie stared at his shirt while he spoke and tried to put from her mind that other sea she had seen, earlier, from the wide window. "Something's wrong," Richmond was saying.

How right you are, Laurie thought.

"We're looking for Ethel Merman here . . ."

Annie peered up at the lights as though looking for someone.

He looked at her sternly. "Be serious, Annie," he said. "I want that Ethel Merman sound."

"From all of us?" Bonnie asked, frowning. An admirer of Joni Mitchell, she wouldn't have been caught dead singing like Ethel Merman.

Richmond thought a minute. "No, just Laurie," he said.

Laurie stared at him. She'd never sung like Ethel Merman.

"But who do *we* sing like?" Annie protested.

"Uh—you two just *sing*."

"And we maintain, like, an Ethel Merman attitude," Annie added. "Is that what you mean?"

"Yeah, that's right," he conceded. Annie always out thought him.

"Well, I don't mean to start an argument or anything," she said, "but if we're supposed to maintain an Ethel Merman attitude, why are we dressed like this?"

"Uh, hum. Well, I don't know."

Laurie groaned and Bonnie elbowed her. When Annie interfered, even though she was often right, things took that much longer. She tried to catch a glimpse of Richmond's watch.

The producer walked up to them; indignation had lengthened his usually pudgy face. "It's Americana!" he almost shouted at Annie. "Don't you people understand? Americana! You're *all* Mrs. Ben Franklin!"

He glared; Richmond patted his back reassuringly; he walked away.

"Okay, I got an idea," Richmond said, glancing at his watch. It was eleven fifteen, Laurie noted, and they didn't even have one take. She hoped she'd have time to go home and change her clothes before the rehearsal. How could she go to her wedding rehearsal—and then a family dinner —in clothes that had spent the night on a strange lover's floor?

"Would you all get down on your knees?" Richmond was saying.

"What?" Laurie whispered.

"Would you kneel, please."

"Is this a house of worship?" Annie demanded.

"No, goddamnit," Richmond said under his breath. "It's an attitude."

The difficult cameraman approached. Laurie saw him coming and set aside another half hour.

"Richmond." He was frowning. "I am very concerned about this scene. The light, it is not subtle." He gestured appropriately. "It has no warmth, it is too hot, it has no golden glow." Here he paused to consider his words. "And then it is also too cold—the blue it has no depth, we are shooting on a flat plane . . ."

"We're not shooting a plane," Richmond yelled. "We're shooting the American flag!"

The cameraman looked down his nose in disgust.

"Now listen," Richmond went on, with another look at his watch. Eleven twenty, Laurie noted. "Let's get this shot . . ."

The cameraman had reached the edge of the lighted area. He turned around. "Richmond, I feel I must tell you what I think of this scene," he said. "These women, they look like Bicentennial, uh . . . Bicentennial nuns." He turned on his heel and walked back to the camera accompanied by titters from his sympathizers on the crew.

Laurie imagined herself all in black, kneeling on a stone floor in a chapel on the other side of the world, condemned to penance for sins of the flesh. But she couldn't think of any prayers, and anyway the floor was dusty. She sneezed. Beside her, with a sigh, Bonnie shifted uncomfortably.

The laughter died down.

"Okay, start crawling toward me as you sing and offer me your waffles," Richmond said. "Okay? Let's go."

The assistant director called for quiet, the mixer for speed, the cameraman for a marker. His assistant ran up, clapped the slate, and they were off.

"Roast 'em! Toast 'em! Put 'em in your oven!
"Eat Mrs. Franklin's waffles every morning!"
"Cut!"

Annie sighed and sat back, rubbing her kneecaps. "Isn't this awfully subservient?" she muttered, to anyone who would listen. "Do you think we should contact N.O.W.?"

"We're trying to re-create an era," Richmond said. "Women weren't liberated in that era."

"Can we get up now?" Bonnie asked plaintively.

"No, not yet." Richmond was lost in thought. "We don't need Ethel Merman here," he mused. "What we really need here is Al Jolson."

The ad agency man strolled over, holding the silver cup from his thermos (he always brought his own coffee). "Richmond, the client expects Ethel Merman," he cautioned.

Richmond thought another moment. "Since we've got an Ethel Merman version in the can, let's put an Al Jolson version on film. It won't cost any more."

"Well, as long as it won't cost anymore, all right." After a look down his nose at the kneeling women the exec went back and sat in his corner.

"Can we get up now?" This time Laurie was asking.

"No, no . . . let's do Al Jolson right from where you are," Richmond said. "Now, forget everything else I told you and just improvise."

"All of us?" Bonnie squeaked, imagining chaos.

"Yeah, I want all of you to think Al Jolson."

"Wait a minute—" Laurie felt confusion overtaking them until three in the afternoon. "So I *sing* like Al Jolson, and Bonnie and Annie maintain the attitude of Al Jolson, is that what you mean?"

"No . . ." Richmond hesitated. "All three of you

sing like Al Jolson . . . 'cause Al Jolson was a guy, right?"

"Right!" Annie yelled furiously. "So all three of us sing *and* maintain the attitude of Al Jolson, right?"

"No. I want Laurie to sing like Al Jolson, and you two guys maintain the attitude of someone who likes waffles."

The three of them exchanged glances and then Laurie squinted up at Richmond's arm to check his watch. It occurred to her that if she was late for the rehearsal, she could always blame it on him. He continued to gaze down at them a moment longer, then turned on his heel and went to consult the cameraman. Laurie sat down on the floor inside the voluminous dress and rested her head on her knees. The costume's musty smell was a comfort. She remembered how she had been all hunched up like that inside a curtain, that afternoon when Manny the bandleader found her on the stage of the Two Pines Social Hall. She was ten. She had taken a guitar from the bandstand and had been crying for hours and hours because she couldn't play it. And then she had confided to him that it was really music she loved, that she hated Larry the Dummy, hated Si. So he had given music to her for a present: lessons, explanations, practice, the only order and discipline in her life, the music that had become her refuge, her means of self-expression, her cure.

Although she wasn't sure what could cure her today. She looked up. Annie and Bonnie had risen and were talking to the two grips at the wind machine. She looked behind the lights at the crew. The cameraman was having his latest say with Richmond; everyone else was just hanging around and drinking coffee. She turned back to the scenery, put her head down again and squinted at the cornfield, which from that angle seemed huge and very far away. She felt as though she were alone in a tall house, looking for miles into the distance. Looking for what? she asked herself, for she had somehow managed to confuse the signals. She was going to live with Kenny, in actual, real-life *marriage*, when all she wanted to do this morning, or any morning for that matter, was to find her way back to Chris's bed, and once again feel the touch of those long fingers.

She looked away from the cornfield to the wood floor of the stage with its half-obliterated chalk marks from past performances, its patina of grime. There didn't seem to be any way out of it: she would go to the rehearsal, she would marry Kenny, she would get a new car. And she would love him because he was kind, and loved her. And the passion of her encounter with Chris she would stow away in her memory until it faded, like her "love" for Rick Tramper had faded. And she would save it there until it came out on a sheet of lined paper: a little chart labeled Words and Music by Laurie Robinson. She traced the five lines of a staff on the floor and a treble clef before them. Without much thought she wrote

"Dd eb, bcc bac," and sang the notes. Then as she looked up at the scenery a lyric came: "So many nights, I sit by my window . . ." The next moment she was off, completely involved in it. By the time Richmond returned and called them back to position she had five lines playing in her mind:

So many nights I'd sit by my window
Waiting for someone to sing me his song,
So many dreams I kept deep inside me,
Alone in the dark,
But now you've come along. . . ." *

"I changed my mind, I think we'll do this next take standing up," Richmond said.

Annie sidled up to Laurie. "You all right, kid? You didn't even move the last five minutes."

Laurie smiled. Sweet Mama Annie. "I'll be okay."

* Copyright © 1977 by Big Hill Music Company

12.

Herman Nussbaum, the former traveling promoter, was Si's oldest and dearest friend. Having left show business in mid-life in search of a profession more suitable for a family man, he had discovered the possibilities of capitalizing on marriage. It was a fortunate discovery because he believed in that institution.

On the strength of this belief he founded Nussbaum's Wedding Palace, and built it into an entrepreneur's dream. With one room fully booked he had added another and then several more, until it was possible on any given Sunday to see five brides almost simultaneously throwing bouquets off identical rococo stairways. And Herman loved his business. Sometimes he would disappear from his wife's side early Sunday morning (she didn't like him to work Sundays anymore, after twenty-five years) to drive down to the Palace and sneak a look. It always thrilled him. His only sorrow was that his son, Harold, showed no interest in the business, and indeed, had so far shown himself hardly capable of inheriting it, when that should happen.

Today Harold was up by the spotlights in the balcony of the Neptune Room. With him were the doves, which were white and in a birdcage and terrified. They weren't a usual complement of Palace ceremonies; Herman had had them flown in from Europe especially to please Si. Harold, who was happiest at the zoo, felt sorry for them and was anxious to let them out, especially the one that looked like it was going to keel over any minute.

He looked over the railing. Below him two lines of people, one of women, one of men, began to file in through the double doors at the back of the room. They continued down a wide red-carpeted aisle banked by folding chairs, toward an altar decorated with elaborate undersea motifs: tridents, seahorses, mermaids, etc. Two long ropes of braided white ribbon were slung over the shoulders of the straining porters; they were pulling a cart on which was mounted a metal replica of a clam, pearlized, and large enough to hold two people sitting upright within it.

At the moment the clam contained Laurie and Ken. It was pitch black inside, and hot. Ken, furious about the whole thing, sat like a stone, which made things a bit easier for Laurie who was having trouble keeping her composure altogether. At first she had wanted to take advantage of the darkness to hold his hand, but her guilt would not permit her. So she sat in numb silence by his side on her ornante, velvet-covered throne, conscious of sitting close to him in clothes that bore Chris's fingerprints, or some other imprint, as yet unnoticed, he had made on her body. She had not had time to go back home and change.

Mr. Nussbaum was directing the procession. "That's it," he called. "Stop! Now . . . bridesmaids . . . extend your left arms on a diagonal. First position. Fingers pointed. That's it. Now ushers . . . extend your right arms . . . to meet the girls . . . that's it. Now form the love archway . . . "

Annie, the lead bridesmaid, made a face.

"Think of it as the sea meeting the sky," he said with tenderness.

Annie groaned. He was a good follow-up to Mrs. Ben Franklin.

"That's it!" Nussbaum cried happily. He left the bridesmaids and ushers to concentrate on the others. "All right, father of the bride . . . move into position."

Si stepped up smartly, his jacket buttoned. Laurie could see him through the clam's side hinge. He looked neat for once, she thought, which was more than she could say for herself.

Nussbaum then called for the groom's parents, Arthur and Clara Rothenberg. Arthur who sold formerly owned Mercedes and Jaguars to stars either rising or declining, and was usually known as Artie the Car King, approached Nussbaum cheerfully as though he were about to make a sale. In fact he had been considering this ever since Nussbaum had confided that he was in a mood to expand again; a fleet of limousines, Artie thought, might add a touch of class to Palace weddings. He planned to spring one on the newly-weds Sunday to let Herman see the scheme work out.

As far as Clara was concerned, the mother of the groom should not have been asked to do a thing. She had a daughter of her own to marry off and figured she'd have enough to do then. But her heart did go out to motherless Laurie, even though Nussbaum's taste rubbed her the wrong way. She strode to the front of the procession look-ing every inch the lady golfer that she was, star-ing straight ahead and thinking not of Sunday's wedding but Friday's party at the pool, which she had graciously consented to arrange.

When everyone was in place Nussbaum con-tinued his directions. "All right now . . . ushers, walk delicate . . . you're like—like creatures of the sea . . . like sea urchins . . . "

The lead usher, a young man who played dou-bles with Ken, shook his head. Whatever he was (and he wasn't always sure), he had definitely never felt like an urchin.

They were halfway down the aisle when Harold called from his balcony perch. The doves were struggling feebly. "Can I let 'em out now, Pop?"

"Not now, you idiot!" Herman yelled. "Just get the lights ready!"

Ken's mother sniffed and looked away. She hoped he'd keep a low profile during the actual wedding. The procession reached the altar at last. Nussbaum pressed a button. Slowly the clam opened until its sides were folded down. Laurie and Ken, momentarily blinded, blinked into the bright lights.

Kenny's jaw was thrust out stubbornly, but only his mother knew what that meant. He stood up. "I am not getting married in a clam," he asserted. "I am NOT getting married in a clam."

"Kenny, you promised . . ." Laurie whispered, pulling at his sweat pants. They had agreed to go through the Wedding Palace for Si's sake, because it was the only way he could put on a "real wedding," which he felt he ought to do for Laurie. Nussbaum was doing it for nothing ("it'll be my present," was what he'd said).

"I know what I promised," Ken growled to Laurie. "But I cannot get married in this clam."

"What's the matter?" Nussbaum turned his myopic gaze on Kenny, whose clenched fists were barely concealed in his sweatshirt pocket.

"Mr. Nussbaum, do you know what it's like riding in this clam? Mr. Nussbaum, it's very noisy," Ken said. "And—"

Leaning in closer to hear him, Nussbaum accidentally pressed the "close" button. The sides of the clam swung up and clanged together over Ken and Laurie's head.

"Mr. Nussbaum, open this clam!" Ken shouted. His voice reverberated inside the metal container and Laurie's ears felt as if she'd been assaulted. She began trembling.

"Listen, Kenny, I'll talk to Si," she managed to whisper as the clam swung open again.

He turned to her angrily. "I've got to *teach* in an hour, so I'll take care of it *now*," he said. "Mr. Nussbaum—" Ken jumped off his throne. "Mr. Nussbaum, you have no idea what its like being in this clam, I mean, this is a VERY loud clam."

"Don't worry, Kenny, we've got that angle covered. The noise the clam makes is always drowned out by the music."

"Great."

"The *wedding* march," Nussbaum chided.

"Mr. Nussbaum, I *know* what kind of music is going to be played at my wedding," Ken insisted. "I just think that this is an extremely loud clam you've got here and I don't want—"

"Well, that's because its motorized," Nussbaum interrupted, indignant by now. What was this young puppy hinting? That he wanted to change the ceremony?

Everyone was fidgeting. "Excuse me," Nussbaum said. "Ushers and bridesmaids, take five." He left to go get a drink of water and one of his stress pills. To ease the tension Mr. and Mrs. Rothenberg led the wedding attendants to a refreshment table.

Ken and Laurie sat down side by side in one of the rows of folding chairs, as though spectators at their own ceremony. "Si, can we see you a minute?" Kenny called

"Sure, what's up?" Si stood in front of them.

"Sit down for a minute, will you?" Ken asked.

"Kenny, what's wrong? What is it?" Si remained standing; he felt more paternal that way.

"Si, I hate the clam," Kenny said.

"What?"

Laurie intervened. "Pop, can you please tell Mr. Nussbaum we don't want the clam?"

"Aw, you're kidding," Si said, "it'll break his heart, can't you just . . . "

There was a commotion behind them and they looked up to see Harold Nussbaum on his way down the aisle. With the doves.

"Uh . . . Arnold," Kenny said, grabbing his arm.

"Harold," the boy corrected, extricating himself resentfully.

"What are those for?" Kenny pointed to the cage.

"We let 'em loose when you say your vows," Harold sneered, as though anyone ought to know that.

"Oh my god." Laurie turned on Si. "Pop—you've got to be kidding, how can . . . suppose they . . ."

But the doves appealed to Si's sense of drama. "Whatdymean?" he said, offended. "He had those doves flown in from Greece!"

The discussion was interrupted at this point by the arrival of Nussbaum himself, who wanted Kenny to help carry something.

When they left Laurie turned to Si. He looked

tired. It was easier for her to worry about him than to think about herself. "What's the matter, Pop, haven't you been sleeping?"

"No, I'm fine—fine," he assured her. "I just need some jokes, I'm working this Moose Lodge in Pasadena . . . "

He had started traveling again after Laurie moved away, even though he was too old to travel, she thought. But he hadn't told her how badly he needed the money. "It's a roast," he explained. "I'm roasting the King Moose."

Only Si could be roasting a king moose, Laurie thought. Aloud she said, "What does he do for a living?"

"He owns a chain of discount carpet stores."

"Hmmn. Discount jokes . . . cheap jokes . . . okay I'm thinking." Laurie closed her eyes

"I've thought of a couple," Si said. "He's so cheap his kids weren't born, they were made in Japan . . . "

"Good, good," Laurie said. "What else, what about his friends?"

"Hasn't got any," Si laughed.

"Well then, how about 'he lays carpet but he screws his friends . . . '"

"Good—I'll use it," Si said.

"Laurie—Si—I need you now," Nussbaum yelled from across the room.

"Okay, Herman, just a minute," Si had his notebook out. "Lays carpet . . . " he started.

Laurie left him writing and hurried over to where she could see Ken glowering in a corner.

He had decided to keep his mouth shut but he wasn't happy about it. He wished he had listened to Laurie in the first place, and had gotten married in city hall. But he hadn't wanted to disappoint his parents either. He was so involved with these thoughts that he barely noticed Laurie as they climbed into the clam and then sat in creaking darkness on their thrones like some absolute monarchs about to be born, while the ushers went through their paces once more and the parents took their places.

But at last they emerged. "Now you two rise." Nussbaum motioned to them. "Okay, Ken, repeat after me: "I, Kenneth Rothenberg . . . ""

"I, Kenneth Rothenberg . . . "

He's really saying it, Laurie told herself, *and I'll have to say it.* A panic of terrible proportions rose inside her . . .

"Take thee, Laurie Robinson—"

"Take thee, Laurie Robinson—"

What would she do? Could she say it? Laurie felt frozen, her mouth stuck together, her feelings displaced by the awful fear . . .

"And so on and so on and so on . . . " Nussbaum said. He wasn't going to finish it. "I now pronounce you man and wife. Now kiss Laurie . . . "

Ken turned to her, his blue eyes blank, his lips thrust out automatically. Where was he, on the tennis court? Laurie stared, unable to respond.

But once again Nussbaum saved her. "No no!" He pulled at Ken's sleeve. "You don't have to kiss her now, it's only a rehearsal . . . "

Kenny turned away, confused, as Nussbaum kept on: Now you wait for the procession to come down from the altar to the clam, and then we let the doves loose—"

The words had hardly left his mouth before there were doves overhead, flying in all directions. Everyone screamed and ran for cover.

"No no, you idiot!" Nussbaum yelled. "I told you no birds today—this is only a rehearsal . . . "

The birds began circling, like a familiar horror movie. Laurie abandoned the clam and crouched between two folding chairs, holding her hands over her head, until she heard Nussbaum call out that the rehearsal was over. She stood up and looked around. Kenny was running his fingers through his hair, convinced he'd been shit on, as his mother approached, cautiously dodging the birds.

"Well," Clara said to Laurie, "your Mr. Nussbaum is putting on quite an extravaganza here, isn't he?" She gazed down her long nose at Laurie.

"You could say that," Laurie said. What did Clara want her to say?

"He and your father have been friends for quite some time?" The tone was icy.

"Yes, ever since Si roasted him," Laurie said, feeling responsible now for Si's defense. And Clara was such a snob . . .

"*Roasted* him?" Clara repeated.

"It's a show-biz term for 'putdown,'" Laurie said, mysteriously she hoped.

"Well, it's nice to have friends," Clara said, but only because Ken was glaring at her.

"Yes it is." Laurie meant that. She looked right at Clara. They had never really become friends. Clara would never give up hoping for someone *really* good enough for her precious Ken.

"I'm just a little worried about this electric shell opening, dear," Clara said, relenting. "You know, you kids could go up in smoke . . . "

The last thing that Kenny wanted was his mother involved. "Don't worry, Mom, it'll be all right, really," he said. Almost to his surprise Laurie squeezed his hand; she was always pleased when he defended her against Clara.

"Well, shall we go then?" Clara said. "We're all having dinner tonight, aren't we?"

"I can't, Mother," Ken said. "I have a late lesson tonight. Didn't Dad tell you I phoned?" He turned to Laurie. "And I tried to call *you* last night but there was no answer."

"Oh . . . I was just—over with Annie . . . "

"I hope you didn't drive home alone in that car of yours," Kenny said. Annie lived in Westwood.

"Oh no, I didn't, someone . . . " Laurie shook her head.

He wasn't really listening. "Okay, well I gotta go." He left a swift kiss near Laurie's ear. "Speak to you later," he said. "Bye," he added to Si, who had come up to them.

Laurie watched her future mother-in-law match his stride as they left the room. He doesn't really need anyone else, was all she could think of.

Then Si's arm was around her and the frayed cuff of his shirt rubbed her cheek. "I tell you, sweetie," he was saying like W. C. Fields, "just use Si Robinson at your wedding and it'll be a smash. How's this—I wouldn't say the groom's mother was pretty and wouldn't say she was ugly, I'd say she was pretty ugly. . . . "

"Si—Jesus . . . suppose she hears you?"

"I can save the show!" he went on, not paying attention. "Without me this whole thing will be just one big clam dip . . . "

"Si!" Laurie broke away from him. "You are *not* performing at this wedding . . . "

"Hey Laur—take it easy . . . "

He hadn't meant it, of course. He was only joking.

"I'm sorry, Pop," Laurie said, patting his arm. "Listen, I've got to go home now and work—on my routine . . . " She always told him she was working on her routine no matter what else she was doing. He complained less that way.

"I was thinking you should get rid of Larry," he said.

"It's not Larry, Pop, it's me."

"What are you talking about?" Si was displaying his loyalty again.

Laurie couldn't take it, not tonight. "I've got to go, Pop, really," she said.

"Why such a hurry? Have a bite with me."

"Maybe tomorrow. Pop, I'm right in the middle of a song . . . "

"A song—I thought you said . . . "

"—and my routine."

"Well, just work on your timing a little more," Si said in his professional voice. "Timing—"

"Is everything," Laurie finished. He was right about that, she thought. He was certainly right about that. The timing of her whole life was *off*. She threw her arms around his neck and kissed him and then was gone.

Si turned back to find Nussbaum. Maybe Herman wanted to have a drink or something. He walked past the open clam. Several as yet uncaptured doves were perched on the thrones. "Say, buddy, is this seat taken?" Si whispered, leering. He leaned on the button and his laughter echoed into the room as the clam banged shut and the astonished birds flew to the ceiling.

13.

The little red car was stuffy with accumulated heat and the seat was burning. Laurie had to spread a tee shirt across it so she could sit down. She opened the windows, but didn't bother putting the top down because all she had in mind was escape, and she was afraid if she took too long leaving Nussbaum's parking lot someone might overtake her. The time gained by her reprieve from dinner was an unexpected boon and she didn't want to waste it.

The Wedding Palace was on Vine Street. Laurie made a quick left, drove by her high school and through their old neighborhood, looking with no particular interest for landmarks, places where she'd spent time. But everything had an air of perpetual unfamiliarity. She remembered when they first came out to Hollywood, feeling slightly cheated, at the absence of very old, small things that to her made a place exciting, gave it depth and mystery, like the hidden graveyard (exactly *seven* stones) behind the movie in the upstate New York town of Flint.

But they had at least stayed still in Hollywood, and for once in her life she'd had her own room. And after a while there was Kenny the first lover she had ever really been friends with, shy Kenny with the fine body that all the girls swooned over. She had swooned too, at first. As the high school bleachers came into view Laurie conjured the Kenny of four years ago, and his sudden embrace beside the football field of that rainy autumn afternoon.

He had been wearing sweat pants that day too. Kenny was okay, she thought, comforting herself. Kenny was exactly the same as he had always been since she had first known him.

But I've changed, Laurie thought. And yet she didn't think that an accurate description either, for much of what she did now was a natural assertion of the Laurie she had always preferred, who had always been there. The music, for instance, and being friends with zany Annie, whom Kenny didn't exactly understand.

The garage under her apartment building on the corner of La Cienega was cool and dark, and the day attendant and the night attendant were laughing together over something on the radio. Laurie rode up in the elevator with the day attendant. She tried to pretend she didn't have the slightest idea that he was going to visit the blonde part-time stripper-singer on the ninth floor who had a fondness for young parking lot attendants. But when she said goodbye to him she couldn't resist a knowing grin and he grinned back, then rolled his eyes at her, and she burst out laughing at this audacious admission of his own lust, which being a young man he didn't take seriously. Nor was anyone else expected to. She laughed all the way to her own floor, the tenth, and was still giggling when she emerged and wondered if it would ever be all right for young women to acknowledge their own fondness for pleasure with such casual bravado.

Except it's not all right when you're getting married Sunday, Laurie reminded herself. But the laughter had relieved her. She no longer felt so bad. It was all over, Chris was gone. Now there was only herself and the night to contend with. And she was home.

When she opened the door the whole room smelled like the varnish on the piano and it was as though she had finally, after a long and perilous journey, reached some safe haven.

Dinner was swift: a can of tuna, two pickles, an apple, juice. She had to keep her weight down anyway. She thought of the huge amounts of food that Kenny required and hoped she wouldn't succumb to eating. After dinner she showered and washed her hair and then sat for a few minutes absolutely still, looking out the window at the faint gray shadows on the horizon that she knew were the distant hills of San Bernardino. The space she could see, limited and framed by her window, reminded her of the cornfield picture in its perspective, the viewer looking down and away into the shadowy distance. Waiting, Laurie thought, for things to happen to you.

And things do happen—

"You just have to work on your timing," she said aloud, in Si's voice. Like last night, like Chris, her whole awesome confrontation with desire. She was sure there could be nothing wrong with something that had felt that right. It was just the wrong time. She got up then and went to her music notebook and carefully sharpened her pencil as Manny with his regard for good tools had taught her. Then she put the blank paper and pencil side by side on the music stand, neatly, struck middle-C, played arpeggios and one of her old songs that she still liked. And then, first with one finger, note by note, and then with chords, writing with the sharp pencil which she resharpened as she went along, she wrote the song. . . For Chris, because of the night he had given her.

"So many nights I'd sit by my window
Waiting for someone to sing me his song.
So many dreams I kept deep inside me,
Alone in the dark,
But now you've come along.
And you light up my life.
You give me hope, to carry on.

You light up my days and fill my night with
  song. . . ." *

The phone rang twice before she heard it.
Laurie looked under the piano bench but it wasn't
in its usual place and then she remembered putting it beside her pillow the night before last after
talking late with Annie.

She scrambled around the piano and dove for
the receiver. It was Jesse, her agent, and he
sounded excited.

"Guess what?"

"What?"

He didn't answer; he was teasing.

"What's up, Jesse?" she almost shrieked. He
only did that when it was something really big.

It was. He had taken her tape to Charley Nelson, the producer of *Pumpkin Face*, who had liked
it very much. They were thinking of dubbing
some music and they might want to use Laurie.
They wanted her to audition tomorrow, Thursday,
at 10 A.M. Could she do it, Jesse wanted to know.

"Ten o'clock?" Laurie repeated. "Charley Nelson?" It sounded too good to be true.

"Now they'll give you a house band—mostly
piano—but bring your guitar too."

"Okay." Laurie was writing furiously.

"And break a leg, honey," Jessie concluded.

Dear Jesse, you never have to be reminded.
"Thanks a lot, pal," she said. "I'll call you tomorrow and let you know how it went."

Dazed, Laurie hung up the phone and went back to the piano. What a break, she thought, but why does everything happen at once? She stared at the penciled sheet in front of her. The second verse was troublesome. She made some changes and then went over it again. Better, she decided. She looked at the clock. It was after nine. A breeze had come up. She opened the window wider and stuck her head out. The gray shadows on the horizon had deepened to black. A purple cloud hung over one faint star. Laurie turned, stretched, sat down on the piano bench again. The next time she looked it was two in the morning and silence had descended on that part of the city.

14.

The anteroom to the sound studio was dim and cool and thickly carpeted. All the people who walked past Laurie to the reception desk were yawning. For once she resembled them: like everyone else a cardboard container of coffee was clutched in her hand. She had ordered it light and sweet to cover the taste and because she thought milk would somewhat mitigate the effects, making her awake enough to sing but not crazy. She had not slept at all. At 2:30 A.M. she had finished the song, but then finding it the best she'd ever written, had decided to sing it for the audition. Why not, she had thought. You don't get a chance to dub a movie every day.Why not risk everything? At 5:40 she had completed a piano score, sketchy but enough for a good musician. Then she had gone to the laundromat, the all-night one on the strip, so that she could go to this audition clean, even if exhausted.

"Miss Robinson?"

Laurie jumped, the coffee sloshed, narrowly missing her clean blouse. She felt as if she were a puppet strung too tight.

But there was a smile and a friendly face where the voice had come from. "Hi, I'm Barbara Claiborne, Charley Nelson's assistant."

"Hi." Laurie put down the coffee and reached to shake her hand. Being met by a young woman about her own age was a relief. She relaxed somewhat.

"You're a little early," Barbara said, with a glance at the clock.

"Oh, I can wait." Laurie backed away, glad of an excuse to put it off, even for a few minutes.

"Oh no, I'm sure it's okay. They're expecting you. C'mon, let's go."

Well, this was it, big chance number one. Clutching her manila envelope of music in one hand and her guitar in the other, Laurie took a deep breath and followed Barbara through the doors marked SILENCE into a cavern of a room where wires snaked in all directions. Complicated couplings, plugs, amps, what seemed like a potentially lethal array of machinery surrounded the musicians and their instruments. Laurie paused, taking it all in, the purple velvet linings of violin cases, cubes of resin, valves, picks, the warm golden glow of a saxophone. How good it felt to be near all this music.

In the control booth a playback was in progress. Barbara gestured at the green-shirted back of someone wearing earphones and whispered "Charley."

Laurie nodded. There was something vaguely familiar about him. But she couldn't place it. He was talking earnestly to the engineers. Barbara waited a respectful moment until he finished, then tapped him on the shoulder.

Charley turned, friendly, with straight half-gray hair. He looked at Laurie as though he too had seen her before but couldn't make the connection.

"Charley, this is Laurie Robinson—and I'm busy. Bye!" Barbara said, and then with a laugh ducked away.

She was on her own. He had his hand out. "Hello," Laurie said. She had to stick the envelope under her left arm to shake his hand.

"Jesse sent your tape over, I liked it very much," he said. He held her hand a moment, still trying to remember where he'd seen her.

"Thanks." Laurie politely withdrew her hand. She had never considered flirting part of the arrangement.

"I guess he told you we're having a problem with the actress for this movie," Charley said. "She, uh . . . can't sing." He looked discouraged. "So we're going to have to dub."

"I understand," Laurie said, in her firmest, all-business kind of voice. It must be the coffee, she thought.

98

"Good." Charley nodded his satisfaction. She seemed competent and sure of herself, although a bit hollowed-eyed. He just hoped she could really sing. "Let's go in and meet the director," he said.

She followed him out of the control booth into the studio, toward the conductor's podium. The musicians were playing, the conductor had his head inclined toward the director, who was speaking into his ear.

"Okay, hold it guys, cut—" The conductor motioned for silence.

"The strings are just way too busy for a love scene," the director said. He turned as he became aware of Charley beside him.

Behind Charley Laurie froze. The shirt on the director was wrinkled blue, not thin brown cotton, but there was no mistaking that body. It was Chris. He was the director of *Pumpkin Face*. *Oh my God,* Laurie thought.

"I hope you don't mind us interrupting, but this is Laurie Robinson," Charley said. "I thought you'd want to—"

"What are *you* doing here?" Chris said, louder than he meant to.

"Pleased to meet you," Laurie said stupidly, because she knew she was supposed to say *something*.

"She's—that singer I was telling you about . . ." Charley looked puzzled. "You know, Jesse sent me her tape . . ."

"I—I didn't know you were a singer," Chris stammered, ignoring Charley.

99

They stood and looked at each other after that, while everyone around looked at *them*. "You two worked together before?" Charley asked, curious now. He still couldn't remember her.

"Once before," Chris said pointedly.

"Yes, once before," Laurie echoed. Oh how dumb and obvious that sounded. She felt herself blushing.

There was a silence. Short but awkward.

"Well, aren't you going to say anything?" Chris demanded.

"What do you want me to say?" She said it quietly, not because of any self-control but because her throat had tightened and she could barely talk.

There was a hot microphone around Chris's neck; he'd forgotten it. The control booth had picked up the conversation and all the engineers were grinning.

"I didn't know you were directing this movie," Laurie said.

"Oh well, yeah . . ." He shook his head. He was still trying to recover from the shock of seeing her just standing there, as though by some miracle he had been suddenly granted a wish to see her again. But it didn't take him long to see that her confusion was even more profound than his own which flattered Chris, made him sympathetic. He also realized that they were the center of attention, and that made him uncomfortable. "Let's talk over here," he said. He led her toward some empty chairs behind the rhythm section, near the red neon exit sign. Laurie looked at it and felt as though she ought to keep on going.

"Did you bring something to sing?"

"Something I wrote." She fished in the manila envelope for the piano score and handed it to him.

"I didn't know you wrote songs, why didn't you . . . "

Laurie shrugged.

He gave her a little searching smile and then began to examine the music. "Who did this chart?"

"I did, but—"

"But what?"

"Well, I don't exactly know what it'll sound like when it's played—I mean by someone who can *really* play . . . "

"Well, I don't know what it'll sound like either, so we'll hear it together." Chris paused. He wanted to reassure her in some way because she looked so tired and nervous, but he didn't know what to say.

Laurie glanced at him, and shook her head slowly. "I don't believe this is happening," she said.

"I don't believe it either." Then he remembered that she had, after all, spurned his attentions, played with his feelings. "Well, let's run one down anyway, okay?" There was a challenge in his eyes.

"Okay." She felt better, meeting his challenge that way. If she could focus her mind on the music everything would be all right. She wouldn't need to think of him. But that was impossible since the song was about him; how could she sing about him without thinking of him? She followed him back to the podium with her head down, picking her way carefully among the wires.

"This is Roy, he'll tell you where to sit. Roy, this is Laurie. Where should she sit?"

She looked up at a kind, seamed face, and the most understanding smile she'd encountered in days. "Oh right there'll be fine," Roy said, indicating a stool near the piano.

Laurie settled herself, watching Roy's reactions to the score as he sat down at the piano and played some chord changes, then called the bass player over, spoke a minute to the drummer. It was all music talk.

"They've been playing together for years," Chris whispered. "They never need to see a score more than once."

Laurie nodded. All she wanted was to get it over with.

"You okay?" He hung in front of her like some specter of another time, another place, a Laurie she couldn't be. She wished he'd go away.

"Listen, just relax and enjoy yourself. I'll be in the control booth." He touched her hand, lightly, but with just enough pressure to remind her that it was Chris Nolan touching her. Then he left.

She looked up to see Roy hovering with the kind of sympathetic, knowing look old musicians often had, an aura of beatitude they carried, as though similar tough situations had sainted them.

102

"Listen, don't worry," he said. "You've probably been scrounging around doing singles and demo sessions, waiting for a break like this. And here it is, so just relax and enjoy yourself. We'll cover you."

"Oh thanks," Laurie said, unconvinced.

"Let me know when you're ready out there." It was Chris's voice, booming suddenly from the booth.

"Oh my God," Laurie said, just as suddenly, and jumped off the stool.

"What's the matter?" Roy looked up from the keyboard, his patient smile still in place.

"I forgot—there's a note here . . . " She reached over him for the spot on the score. "You see it's an octave low—I forgot to change it."

"Oh, good," he said. "That's just fine. Okay." He noted the change with a pencil but she could tell he wasn't paying attention because he already had his mind on the music as a whole, and one change was just one change.

"Oh, and it's three-quarter time," she said.

"Yeah, we saw," the bassman said, smiling. His smile said sit down girlie, and sing. We do this all the time.

Laurie slouched back to her seat and resolved to sit there and breathe, like Manny taught her. *Relax*, she thought. *I do this all the time.*

"Ready out there?" Chris called. "What's the name of the song?"

"You—" Laurie faltered, turned away to clear her throat. Yes *you,* she thought, and turning

back said into the mike clearly this time: " 'You
Light Up My Life.' "

" 'You Light Up My Life,' " Chris repeated.
"Okay, here we go, take one."

So many nights I'd sit by my window
Waiting for someone to sing me his song.
So many dreams I kept deep inside me,
Alone in the dark,
But now you've come along.
And you light up my life.
You give me hope, to carry on.
You light up my days and fill my nights with
  song.
Roll in at sea, a-drift on the waters,
Could it be fin'lly I'm turning for home.
Fin'lly a chance to say, "Hey! I love you."
Never again to be all alone.
And you light up my life.
You give me hope, to carry on.
You light up my days and fill my nights with
  song.
You light up my life.
You give me hope, to carry on.
You light up my days and fill my nights with
  song.
It can't be wrong when it feels so right,
'Cause you, you light up my life.*

15.

The applause exploded over the mikes in the control booth.

"She's *really* good," Chris whispered.

"Good? Good's not the word, man, she's dynamite."

"With a little more echo, and some strings ... "

"I've *seen* her," Charley said. "In a couple of commercials, I think. But I thought I remembered her from someplace else."

"You saw her with me the other night at Casey's."

"Oh *yeah*." Charley grinned. "I thought she looked familiar. You didn't know she could sing?"

Chris shook his head, shrugged.

"I wonder ... " Charley paused. "You think she can *act*?"

"I'm way ahead of you," Chris said. "It's worth a shot. Hand me that script."

Laurie was surrounded by a cluster of musicians congratulating her and offering advice. If you need arrangements honey, go to John Bellson," Roy was saying. "He's the best."

"I just want to tell you I enjoyed that, child." It was the old sax man, who could have been seventy, and who had played behind her after he'd found the tune, adding another voice and so another dimension to the song, to Laurie's delight.

"Oh listen, thank you," she said, reaching to shake his hand. "But if I'd rehearsed it, I could have done much better." Holding his dry, knotted hand, she kissed him respectfully on the cheek. But then, lascivious to the end, he winked at her.

Everyone laughed. Chris arrived then and after instructing Roy to give the men ten, led her away again to the corner behind the rhythm section. "You were terrific," he said. "But you know that, don't you?"

"Not really."

He dismissed her modesty. Not knowing her, he saw no reason for her not to feel sure of herself. "Let me ask you something," he went on. "Can you act?"

Laurie was silent, looking at him. What was he asking? "I'm an actress, if that's what you mean," she said.

"How are you at cold readings?"

"About as good as I am at cold singing I guess."

"That's what I was hoping you'd say. Come with me, I want you to read something." He practically yanked her out of the chair and held her arm all the way to the control booth as though he were afraid she'd run away if he let go. They entered to renewed applause from Charley and the engineers. Laurie was pleased but dazed. Things were happening too fast to absorb—especially on no sleep.

"Uh, can we use this room for a few minutes, guys?" Chris eyed Charley.

Charley nodded, then herded the others out.

"Have a seat," Chris said, when they were alone.

"What the hell is going on here?" Laurie said, sitting down cautiously.

With a professional glare Chris looked her straight in the eye. "What the hell's going on here is that you're reading for my movie," he said. "Here's the script, turn to page twenty-two."

"You're really directing this movie," Laurie said. She hadn't quite believed it. Now there was the evidence—*Shooting Script, Pumpkin Face*—right in her hand.

"Yeah, I'm the director, unless I've been fired in the last half hour," Chris said, amused by her disbelief.

But something else had impressed her. "How come you know so much about music?" she demanded.

"Why are you asking me all these questions?" He was sitting opposite her and bent forward suddenly and gave her a quick light kiss. A little tease. A little reminder.

Oh don't, Laurie thought. She looked at him reproachfully.

"I know about music because I used to produce records," he said, becoming serious again. "Okay, back to business—here's the place in the script."

"Just this speech?" It was only a paragraph.

"From here . . . to here."

When he bent toward her this time she stiffened and moved away. "Can you give me some directions?"

"Okay." He sat back, concentrating, very professional. "The scene takes place in a bar," he said, "the kind of bar that would scare the hell out of most anyone else, but to you it's home, it's like family. Your father was a drinker, he was even a drunk, and the only way you got out of it was with humor. Here there is contact made when you're talking to a guy who's really tough. You're even a little drunk yourself, but don't emphasize that in your reading. Okay?"

"I think so," Laurie said. The piece was about trains, she had all sorts of associations with trains. It didn't seem hard. "Are you going to read with me?"

"Will that throw you?"

Laurie paused before she answered and looked at him gravely, thinking he'd already done it, she could hardly be thrown any further. Then, impatient that her private feelings could overcome her professionalism, she said, "No, it's okay if you read, anyway let's just try it."

They did. It worked well. When she finished

they sat in silence a moment, caught in the spell of the scene and the intimacy of the control booth, a place of honest feeling; they both were aware that music doesn't lie.

"That was very good," Chris said finally, in a soft voice.

"Thank you. That direction you gave helped a lot." She laughed, almost bitterly he thought for someone her age. "By the way it's true," she said, referring to the scene, "I don't like trains."

"Why?"

"Because my mother died on one. We were on the road . . ." She looked at him. "Did I tell you my father was a stand-up comic?"

"No, you didn't." You didn't tell me anything, his eyes said.

Laurie looked away. "Well we were on the train and she died—a massive stroke—and then we rode to Poughkeepsie, that was the next town . . . and then we buried her." She looked up to find him right *there* with her, sympathetic and interested, ready to hear more. But she jumped up and handed him the script. "Hey listen, I've taken up enough of your time. Your ten minutes is almost up." She pointed at the clock.

He smiled. "You can't take enough of my time," he said, but he got up anyway. "C'mon, I'll walk you out."

They met Barbara and Charley at the studio door. Chris gave him the script. "She was fabulous," he said. "I'll talk to you later."

109

Charley gave him a knowing grin. "I only bring talented people in," he said.

Laurie tucked the music envelope under her arm and reached to shake Chris's hand. "Listen, thanks for everything." She meant it.

He squeezed her hand tight. "Well, destiny keeps bringing us together," he said.

"Wait a minute—I thought *I* brought you together," Barbara said.

Everyone laughed, which made it that much easier to leave.

"Wait for me, we'll have lunch together," Chris said suddenly, as they were walking toward her car.

"I can't. You know I can't."

"Why not? It's just *lunch*, for God's sake. I want to talk about the *film*. As soon as possible."

Laurie fiddled with the adhesive on the car roof. Damn, she would have to see him now, it was a question of business. No matter how she felt. But she had to sleep first.

"I have errands to run now," she said. "But— maybe later. Tonight's all right I guess."

"Do I have to get your number from Charley Nelson—or will you give it to me this time?" He had his pencil out.

Laurie blushed. "482-7262," she mumbled.

"Talk to you later then. Take care." He patted the rounded front fender of the little red car as though he were patting Laurie, glanced at his watch, and ran.

Driving home she noticed it was only twelve

110

noon. Most of the bars were still closed, a few retail stores were just then opening and their owners out sweeping sidewalks. Laurie felt as though it were still morning too, but all she could think of was sleep. She turned the radio on so loud to keep awake that the day attendant put his hands over his ears when she drove into the garage. He had circles under his eyes too, she noted.

In the apartment everything was just as she left it: pieces of scrap paper all over, a half-finished glass of juice staining the piano bench. Laurie threw her clothes across the room and fell into bed but then she lay there wide awake and went over every aspect of the morning and then back through the last three days. There was Kenny to think of, and Si. The Rothenbergs, though she didn't really like them. She tried to be moral, she tried to be rational. But she fell asleep confused.

16.

At night the lighted tennis courts always reminded Laurie of movie sets as she approached them, with the little white figures of the players moving so swiftly and purposefully they seemed set in motion not by their pursuit of the ball but by some unseen director's design. "Life's a game of tennis," she could hear Si saying, "just be sure to hit the ball—it's a matter of timing."

She moved into the right hand lane to make the turn into the first driveway but then saw there was no one behind her and pulled to the left again. "Maybe I oughtn't to go in at all," she thought. "I'll just upset him if I do." But she wanted reassurance. Desperately. She had spent so little time with Kenny this past week that in a way she no longer knew who he was. They had not held each other or been to bed, it seemed, for ages. He did not feel like her *lover*. When she thought about sex she could only think of Chris. Laurie felt as though she'd gotten on a wrong train and couldn't remember any of the connections to the right one.

Without looking properly she pulled into the right lane again and got a loud horn and a nasty look as a sleek Mustang pulled up and passed her. *Jesus, if I don't watch out I'll get myself killed,* she thought. It occurred to her that might be a way out of the whole dilemma anyway. Still she was more careful making the turn into the second driveway, and as she pulled into the lot.

She cut the motor and sat a minute, still deciding whether to go in. It was eight o'clock and the sky was a pale romantic gray. Her date with Chris was for eight thirty at his studio office. (His call at five had awakened her; he teased, then confessed he'd had a nap too. He was meeting her at his office only because she had refused to come to his house.)

So there was really no reason to bother Kenny. Although she would have had to drive past the courts anyway. Still there was no reason. . . .

"Yes there is a reason," she said aloud, and yanking the keys out of the lock, she ran across the yard to the low concrete-block office building.

All eight courts were filled. Kenny was teaching at the end, his pupil a middle-aged divorcée Laurie recognized as a friend of his mother. She felt a twinge of entirely inappropriate jealousy.

"Could you please page Kenny Rothenberg?" she said to the receptionist.

"He's giving a lesson." For emphasis the girl snapped her gum.

"I know . . . it's important," Laurie insisted.

"Oh, you're Laurie, right?"

She nodded.

"Okay." The girl pushed the intercom. "Kenny Rothenberg, court one. Come to the office, please."

Laurie paced, watching Kenny's progress through the series of fences. He looked startled when he saw her. "Honey, what are you doing here?" he asked. He gave her a little peck on the cheek; he was dirty and she looked so fresh and clean. As though she just got up, he thought, without the least idea that he might be right. Kenny kept regular hours.

"I'm sorry to bother you," Laurie said, when she saw him glance at the large wall clock and then out at court one, where Mrs. Levy lounged against the net post, tapping her foot.

"No, that's okay, it's no bother," he said. "What's up, hon?"

"I—I don't know," Laurie lied sadly. "I'm feeling sort of—depressed."

"Why?"

The receptionist's ears turned red although she respectfully pretended to read her magazine.

"Because—I don't know," Laurie said.

"Ah, it's just pre-wedding jitters. You want me to come over tonight?" Teasing, he pulled her hair over her nose.

She would have gladly said yes but she didn't know what time she'd get back, or how she'd feel. "What I would like is for you to hug me *now*," Laurie said.

"Aw c'mon Laur, I'm all sweaty."

"Please hug me, Kenny."

He took her in his arms and was surprised to find her shaking. She clung to him. That was unlike her. "What's all this?" he asked.

"I'm just trying to hold onto you," Laurie whispered.

"But I'm not going anywhere."

"I know."

"But, Laurie, you're shaking." He held her at arms length, the way she had seen him inspect a racquet. "C'mon, what's the matter?"

"I'm just a little scared, I'm . . . on my way to an audition. This director—he heard me sing this morning, and I may get a part . . ."

"But that's incredible—you should be happy! Is that what you came to tell me?"

"Do you love me, Kenny?" Laurie asked abruptly, not even caring that the receptionist was gazing at them now, openly entranced.

"Of course I love you, Laurie," he said. He managed to appear worried about her and impatient at the same time.

"But do you *really* love me?"

He glanced out at the court again and then looked back at her, frowning. "Laurie, what's the matter with you tonight?"

"I don't know."

"I've got to get back."

"Okay." There was no use in it, she thought. "I'll be okay, Kenny," she said.

"Do you want me to hug you again?"

"Yeah." She leaned lightly into his arms as he patted her. For a jock, it was really a feeble excuse for a hug, the receptionist thought.

"Have a good audition," he said.

"Tell me to break a leg."

"Oh yeah, break a leg." Halfway out the door he turned, feeling suddenly obliged to display more responsibility for her, especially in front of the receptionist. "By the way," he said, "do you have enough gas in the car?"

"Yes." She felt like a child when he said that. Anger began to fill the hollow in her stomach.

"I want you to get rid of that car," Kenny said importantly.

"Okay, Kenny, okay."

"I mean it, Laurie," he said. "I want you to start thinking about a new car for yourself, all right?"

"All right, Ken." She glanced at the court. Mrs. Levy looked pissed. "You better go now."

"Okay, goodbye, I'll see you tomorrow afternoon."

"What?" She'd forgotten.

"The *party*, dummy." He grinned. "You *do* have the jitters."

"Oh, of course." She smiled. He didn't know it was a smile of dread. "Oh goodbye, Kenny," she said.

17.

There was an accident on Sunset Boulevard; she was fifteen minutes late and edgy when she arrived. Going to see Kenny had been stupid, Laurie decided. Now she just felt worse. She was hoping an engineer might be around so she wouldn't have to be alone with Chris.

The studio building wasn't empty—a guard sat at the lobby desk reading *Playboy* and several executives were having a whispered conference near a phone booth. But Laurie was alone in the elevator and when she stepped into the dark carpeted hallway of the third floor she realized she felt just as threatened here as she would have at Chris's house.

He was sitting in the otherwise deserted reception area with his feet on the desk, reading *The New York Times*. He looked over the paper as the elevator doors opened. "Ah, the composer arrives," he said.

"I'm sorry I'm late, there was an accident. . . ."

He smiled. "I was going to give you an hour," he said, "and if you chickened out . . ."

"I wouldn't do that."

"No, you probably wouldn't." He stuffed the newspaper into a wastebasket and with a yawn unfolded himself from the chair. "Paper puts me to sleep," he said. "But I read it so I won't get homesick."

"You miss New York?"

"Yes." He looked thoughtful as he led her along the hall toward his office.

"Does your wife live there?"

"More questions, eh?" He grinned, glad of the curiosity that betrayed her interest. His own interest in her hadn't diminished. He liked her lips a lot. He waved her into a comfortable seat but she sat instead on the stool in front of his small electric piano. He got them some drinks from a cooler and then sat across from her. "To answer your question," he said. "She's my ex-wife, really. We haven't lived together in quite a while." His eyes got faraway and she sensed some disappointment in his life. "But it's not her I miss," he went on, "it's everything else. "You ever live there?"

"Not in the city very often, but all around. Wherever my father played."

"You ever think of going back?"

Laurie laughed, shrugged. "About six months

ago I had a chance to," she said. "I had an offer from Columbia. It was pretty firm, but—I would've been there a while . . ."

"How come you didn't take it?"

"I had just been engaged."

"Oh."

"Jesse tells me the door's still open there, but I don't know . . ."

They were silent, sympathetic in some common recognition of how people can be caught between opportunities. "Well," Laurie said, with a 'that's show-biz' kind of a shrug. "Can I use this piano?"

"Sure."

While they set up the piano and got the music arranged he told her that he and Charley were having a meeting with the executive producers and that they wanted to supplement the tape they'd made of her first audition with a tape of her singing alone.

She sang "You Light Up My Life" once lightly, to warm up.

"Okay, start again," he said. "This time I'm going to be critical."

She got halfway through before he stood up. "Uh—hold it a minute." He went to the cooler. "Can I get you something else—a beer maybe? Soda?"

"No thanks, I'm not thirsty," Laurie said. "What's the matter with the song?"

"Well—"

"You don't like it," Laurie said. "I thought you liked it."

He shook his head, took a sip of his beer before he answered. "No, you're wrong," he said. "I love your song and I love your voice, but—"

She waited, feeling anxious while he gathered his thoughts. Taking criticism was always so difficult.

"It's the reading you give that song," he said finally. "Do you believe those words you're singing?"

Oh god, Laurie thought. "Well I wrote them," she said. "Of course I believe them."

"Well then how come I don't?"

"I don't know."

"You've got to *bleeeeed* a lyric," he said. "Right now I feel like you're just singing the words. Like you were demonstrating notes."

He got up and went to the window, and toyed with the curtain pull. "All right, now let me hear it again, from—" He checked the music in his hand. "From 'Rollin at sea . . .'"

> Rollin at sea, a-drift on the waters,
> Could it be fin'lly I'm turning for home.
> Fin'lly a chance to say 'Hey! I love you.'
> Never again . . .*

"Okay, wait a minute, look try it this way." He squeezed beside her on the piano bench and reached across her for the chords. She hadn't known he could play.

Fin'lly a chance to say 'Hey! I love you!'
Never again to be all alone . . .*

He stopped, fiddling with the treble. "How do you know my song so fast?" Laurie demanded, half angry and half amazed.

"That's what I *do*." He smiled. He always liked letting his talents out little by little. "Do you see what I mean, though," he went on, turning to her. "You're telling someone this story. It's not every day you get a chance to say 'I love you.' When you sing the words 'I love you,' all the heartbreak that went *before* has to be there. I mean, that's what makes love so good. It erases all the pain." He looked into her eyes, wondering if she was old enough to understand all that. "Do you know what I mean?"

"I think so." At that moment Laurie thought she understood a great deal about pain.

"Try it again."

She sang.

"Much better," he said when she'd finished. "Still not all the way, though."

Laurie, used to accolades for her music, looked downcast. And besides, she knew her singing sounded insincere because she didn't want it to sound otherwise. But he was challenging her—almost daring her, she thought, to do it right. The next time she gave out more: "Fin'lly a chance, to say 'Hey! I love you!' " . . .*

"Good. Let's just make a technical adjustment. Try it more 'throaty.' It's an intimate moment. Sound like you mean it, more like this." He came up into her face and said softly "Hey! I love you!"

Laurie would not look at him. But the next time she sang the way she knew he wanted to hear it. The way she felt it.

Chris hadn't expected to find himself so moved. "That's it," he said softly. "I really felt that you meant it."

"I do," she said, compelled to say it now. "I do mean it, do you?"

"I mean it," he said, though in truth he did not know what he meant.

Laurie got up from the piano bench and went to the window. The sky was black, the lights of L.A. crisp against it. *Oh, what have I said, what have I done, what do I do now?* "I didn't want this to happen," she said.

"I know you didn't." He came up behind her and reaching around her waist pressed her to him. "You should have tried harder."

She turned then and put her arms around his neck and welcomed the kiss he offered. Then she rested her head against the hollow of his neck, glad just to be there. "Listen," she whispered, "whatever happens I want you to know that I do love you."

He held her away from him with his long fingers pressing her shoulders. "It's still early," he said. "Let's make a good tape quick, and when we get to my place we can take a walk on the beach."

Laurie was silent.

"If you want to," he said.

She looked at him. Nothing in the world could have made her refuse.

18.

When Laurie arrived at her door without calling the next morning Annie knew right away something was wrong. "Why aren't you home resting up for the party?" she asked.

"I'm on my way there now but, Annie, I haven't been home since yesterday." Laurie ran a hand over her eyes.

At the sight of her Jerry's two boys shot through the doorway. Jackie was eight and Eric ten, and together they seemed to be all arms and legs and requests for the gum she usually brought them.

"Don't worry, I didn't forget you guys." Laurie reached in her bag and brought out a package for each, and even managed a smile.

"Nothin for me?" Jerry was in the living room about to leave, with a guitar under each arm. "Hi Laurie, goodbye," he said good-naturedly. "I've got a session at three but I'll be back for the party. Wouldn't miss it."

"See you later," Annie said as he kissed her. "Did you get my note about the session at United tomorrow? They want you on twelve-string electric."

"I got it, thanks. Bye."

"Bye." They watched him run down the walk, past the kids who were sitting on the front porch, very involved in chewing. "All right, what happened," Annie said as soon as Jerry was out of earshot.

Laurie covered her eyes again. "Oh, Annie—" She didn't even know where to start.

"Wait—I gotta keep an eye on the kids. Come sit outside."

The boys went down the block to play with friends. Laurie sat down on the wooden porch steps. Annie's house always reminded her of Brooklyn. Annie yelled something to the boys and then sat down beside Laurie, squinting into the sunshine.

"Why are you holding your face up like that?" Laurie asked.

"Trying to get a little tan to match my peach dress. I'm wearing it to the party." She turned, stared at Laurie. "You could use a little sun too," she said. "You look pale as a ghost." She called something to Jackie.

"You really love those kids, don't you," Laurie said. She wondered if she could ever mother anyone—Annie did it so easily.

"Yeah, I love them," Annie said. "Jerry and the kids have made my life a lot of fun."

"You guys are really lucky."

"Don't I know it." Annie hadn't always been lucky. "But what's the matter, Laurie?" Annie said finally.

She began with the good parts first. "They're thinking of using my voice for the songs in *Pumpkin Face*."

"That's great!"

"I might get the lead."

"You're kidding! I thought Carla Wright had it!"

"No, it's still open, I read for it. I may get it. Chris said they'd decide in a day or so."

"Chris who?"

"Chris Nolan, the director. Annie, he—"

"Laurie? Just tell me what happened."

Bit by bit, through tears, Laurie told her the whole story, ending with their late night walk on the beach and the perfect love they had made afterward.

"But I just don't understand how you let yourself get into this mess," Annie said when she had finished.

"Oh Annie, didn't you ever have a handsome man come up to you and look into your eyes and grab you and kiss you . . ."

"Uh, no," Annie said, deadpan. "That never happened."

"Oh, Annie, don't make jokes," Laurie protested.

126

"But Laurie, the *wedding* party's this afternoon . . ."

"Oh, I don't *want* a party, I don't even know if I want a wedding . . ." Laurie put her head down and began to cry softly into her knees.

"You're sure all this doesn't have anything to do with the part?" Annie asked suspiciously.

"Of course not," Laurie sobbed.

Absently Annie patted her, a bit dubious and still too amazed to offer advice, and hoping that she'd still have a chance to wear her peach-colored dress with the embroidered roses on it.

19.

Kenny's mother had arranged for the party to be set up on the lawn. There were three tents. The two on either side of the flower-filled pool were for dancing and the third, set slightly behind and nearer the house, was for use as a kitchen cum bar. There was much scurrying around on the part of numerous white-jacketed waiters; smells wafted, smoke rolled. The dance tent emitted a continuous if muted throb: Arthur Rothenberg had declared, rather abruptly, that if he paid for the party he also had a say in the music, and he wasn't having that damn clamor of rock in his ears for four hours.

Although it was slightly larger and fancier than the usual, the party didn't differ too much from other parties the Rothenbergs had given during the time Laurie had known them. In fact, as she and Si walked around in Clara's wake being introduced to relatives, she kept feeling as if it were really Ken's sister's graduation party, which she had attended two years before. Clara was so experienced that she always did things *right*, which after a while came to mean *the same*. One always knew what there would be to eat and drink at a Rothenberg fest and little besides the color of the decorations changed.

"Oh Clara, what a lovely idea—to give a party *before* the wedding!" someone gushed. Laurie looked up to see a buxom woman in a red dress.

"Cousin Georgiana!" Clara cried. "And Uncle Fritz—and Cousin Judith!"

Laurie nodded. Smiled. Within her, a strange inner fog, a disbelief, rejection. She kept looking around for Ken. He and his father were lagging behind the introductions; they both knew better than to keep up.

"Laurie—this is your new uncle Leonard—Leonard, this is Laurie and her father, Si."

Hellos were exchanged. Si caught sight of the bar, which had eluded him for a few minutes. He planned to spend a little time in front of it if he could just get away from Clara . . .

Ken caught up. "Listen, Laurie, Murray and Gail are back at the house, so I'm just gonna go over for a minute and say hello. . . ." He started to leave before she could even say anything to him.

"Oh Ken—" Si called him back.

"Yeah?" Impatience sparked Kenny's eyes.

"Looks like your florist blew up in the pool," Si joked, pointing at the flowers.

Laurie cringed. Ken didn't really get the joke. "Uh—I'll get back to you, Si," he said, and disappeared.

"Gee, you're sure in a good mood today," Laurie said. She sounded almost surly herself.

"And why not!" Si exclaimed. "I knocked the Moose Lodge dead last night!"

"Pop, that's great!"

"Yeah, I killed every Moose in the joint."

"What worked?" Laurie said, automatically thinking show-biz.

"Everything!" Si waved his empty glass. "Oh I was really rollin'—oh, you know, the autopsy proved negative, the wax in his ears, the eternal flame . . ."

"How about 'he lays carpet but he screws his friends?' "

"The biggest laugh of the *night!* Oh I set 'em up and popped it, and BLAM! Knocked 'em dead!" Si turned exuberantly and bumped into an attractive but amazed couple at the bar. "A toast to the bride!" he cried into their startled faces.

Glasses were filled, raised, drained. The attractive couple left for the dance floor. Laurie took a sip of her drink and then turned away, thinking she'd go back to the house and find Ken. She just wanted to be near him.

But Si was in front of her, frowning. "What's the matter?"

"Nothing."

He knew better. "Ah, don't let all their ugly relatives get to you," he said. She didn't respond. "Hey, is it the shell?" he asked. "I'll talk to Nussbaum, there's still time."

"It's not the shell, Pop," Laurie said. "It's nothing."

"It's the routine. It's still not working."

"Pop, I'm fine," Laurie said.

"Maybe you should get rid of the dummy."

"Si—please." With relief Laurie saw Annie approaching. "Si—why don't you ask Annie to dance?"

"Laurie, something's the matter," he insisted.

"Ah, c'mon Si—"

Annie winked at Laurie, and crooking her finger, beckoned to Si. "Aw Si, I'm so lonely," she purred, taking his hands.

Si gave in. They disappeared into the dance tent and Laurie began to nod and smile her way toward the house. She found Kenny on the front lawn in conversation with a tall thin woman rather obviously potted.

"This is Laurie, Aunt Emma," Kenny said.

"I was just telling Kenneth he shouldn't teach here," she said. "He should teach in Miami so I'd see more of him."

"I see enough of you when you're here, Aunt Emma," Ken said.

"Aw don't tease your little old aunt!" She leaned tipsily down at Laurie. "What's your name, dear?"

"Laurie."

"You're okay, Laurie." She waved her glass in

the air. "All right, who's gonna get me a drink?" she said loudly.

"Oh let me, Aunt Emma." Ken grabbed the glass out of her hand and ran for the bar.

Laurie tried to follow him but was intercepted by Si and Annie, who had finished dancing. Both of them were out of breath. "I'm going to get something to drink," Annie said. "Anybody want anything?" She gave Laurie a long look.

"No thanks," Laurie said.

"Okay, I'll see you. Here, Si, take care of my hat!"

"Hey, that's what I call the last straw!" he called after her. Laurie grimaced. "Annie's a funny kid," he said.

"Yeah," Laurie said absently.

"You're sure you're not mad at me because of Nussbaum and the doves and the shell . . ."

"I told you *no*, Si. Why do you keep asking me?"

"Because I know you, Laurie," he said gently.

"Si, believe me, everything's going to be okay."

"Oh boy—now we're *really* in trouble."

Laurie glared at him.

"Because if everything were gonna be all right, you wouldn't say anything. You'd be out there having a good time."

Laurie turned to watch Aunt Emma at the bar.

"Do you love him?" Si asked.

"Who?" Laurie asked, confused. "You've got a real treat in store, meeting Aunt Emma," she added to cover herself.

"Laurie, do you love Ken?"

Angrily Laurie turned on him. "Of course I love him—why do you ask me something like that?"

"You haven't danced with him once."

"He doesn't like to dance."

"You haven't even touched him."

"Pop—there are people around."

"When your mother and I were engaged we couldn't keep our hands off each other."

"You were a lech," Laurie said fondly.

"At *our* engagement party—and that was when people were still 'old-fashioned'—we left the dance floor and went into the bathroom and made love—right there on the cold floor with all the other fools down at the party."

"You're kidding," Laurie said.

"Hey, what am I, chopped liver?" Si said airily. "After all, I used to be quite an attractive man."

"You still are."

"Laurie." He looked at her, hesitated. "Laurie —I know we never had a real home, and it wasn't always good. . . ."

"Hey, man! It was the best," Laurie said.

"Well—I just want you to know that I don't need all this, you know—I know someday the jokes'll be gone and the roast'll be over—" He suspected that somewhere in her subconscious she was marrying Ken so he, Si, wouldn't have to worry about money.

"Si, I love you to pieces, but you're crazy," Laurie said.

"Yeah, crazy like a fox," he insisted.

"You know you shouldn't drink, because you can't handle it."

"Whatdyamean," Si said. "I had two little celery tonics . . ."

Ken arrived. "Come meet Uncle Henry," he said, taking her hand.

"Don't forget the bathroom floor." Si felt it was a last-ditch effort.

"What'd he say?" Ken asked.

That was all Si heard of them. He asked himself if he were drunk and got a negative answer, but there was a strange look on his face as he watched them go. He wished he could guide her more, but in matters of feeling he had always thought Laurie needed a woman's advice. Besides, she was supposed to be grown, although that fact didn't seem to alter his wanting to protect her. He felt somewhat at a loss, and with a shrug went to give back Annie's hat.

20.

Laurie lay in bed without moving, as though her grief were a stone that had weighted her down and immobilized her. Tissues were scattered on the bed, on the floor—hours of tissues, for she had lain this way a long time. At three the piano was an unseen hulk in the night, by five when the sky had lightened, the mahogany's first brown glow appeared above her, and though she could not really welcome the day she felt relieved that the worst night of her life was over.

She had known since midnight that she would have to do it. The decision had almost made itself, because of the dance floor, which after the party Kenny had had to help dismantle. Clara insisted that the floor come up immediately lest it ruin the lawn, because the National Grass Court Singles were being held there the following week.

Laurie had asked Kenny to take her home. She knew if he did he would stay; she hoped if he stayed she could fall in love with him again and wipe out everything else that had happened—or at least set it aside. Make it into another song. But then Kenny had not come with her; he was used to listening to Clara and he listened. And it had been the last straw.

Having decided at midnight she had immediately phoned Chris. There was no answer. She phoned again at two. *But it's Friday night*, she thought, *he has a right to be out partying*. Still she felt anxious, and let the phone ring ten times before she hung up.

At six the sun appeared over the hills of San Bernardino, a red-gold crescent, then a ball in the light blue sky. Laurie waited until all the objects in the room were discernible and she was surrounded by the clear shape of every familiar thing. Then she rose, poured a glass of juice, and called Si. He was never an early riser but he woke up fast when she told him.

The final wedding rehearsal was at noon. Laurie got to Nussbaum's late because after talking to Si exhaustion overcame her and she had fallen asleep. She was still groggy now when she turned into the lot. Kenny's car was already there, as well as a number of others she recognized.

The wedding party was hanging out at the back of the aisle, a few of the attendants lounging on the open clam with its vacant thrones as though they were court jesters waiting for their jobs to begin. With a wave and a "Hi!" that she hoped sounded normal Laurie passed them and ducked around to the side aisle. Kenny was at the altar, in a tête-à-tête with Nussbaum. She walked slowly toward them, so rigid with tension that she felt she might break.

"Look, Ken—I've tried everything," Nussbaum was saying. "I've even changed the birds, and I put the people boy-girl-boy-girl . . ."

"Look, Mr. Nussbaum," Ken interrupted, "I don't *care* if you've put them boy-girl-boy-girl. *Please*—as a favor to me—*no clam.*"

Nussbaum sighed. *Headstrong, these spoiled boys,* he thought. "Okay," he agreed. "But we'll have to practice some new moves immediately."

"Mr. Nussbaum, you're a prince." Ken looked up to see Laurie and began waving her toward him.

Nussbaum strutted up the aisle, wounded but still in command.

"Laurie—I got a surprise! Guess what? I convinced Nussbaum to axe the clam! C'mon—he wants to show us our new moves." He took her hand to lead her up the aisle.

He was so eager that for a moment Laurie almost abandoned her resolve. But she sat down instead. "Wait a minute, Kenny, please. I want to talk to you."

"C'mon Laur, we'll talk afterwards. We gotta get with him now for these moves, or he'll kill us . . ." He yanked at her hand.

Laurie sighed. Ever obedient Kenny. "Kenny, I have to talk to you *now*," she said.

He noticed for the first time that she seemed not her nervous self of the past week but strangely withdrawn. "Okay, what's up?" he said, sitting down beside her.

Laurie swallowed once, then she said it. "I can't marry you, Kenny."

"What?"

"I can't marry you." Said twice, it was irrevocable.

"What are you talking about?" Kenny's disbelief was so thorough he could only feel impatience. She was holding things up. "Hey c'mon—you're just nervous," he said, patting her shoulder.

"But I don't love you, Kenny," she protested. All at once she felt desperately the need to be honest with him. "It's not the way it should be," she said, and then thinking of Chris added: "Not the way it can be . . ."

He just stared at her.

"When you think about it, Kenny, do you really love me?"

"Of course I love you." Was she crazy?

"No you don't, Kenny. You don't."

"Would I be sitting here right now, waiting to marry you, if I didn't love you?" He looked hurt and forlorn, like an abandoned boy.

"That's just why I can't marry you," she burst out, replying less to his statement than to the way he looked, so young and innocent, so unaware of the Hollywood Laurie, music-woman, sensualist.

"When did all this happen?" Ken said. He was dazed.

"I don't know. Maybe it's been happening for a long time."

"Hey—would you go for a giant chrysanthemum that opens?" It was Nussbaum calling down the aisle.

"Not now, Mr. Nussbaum, not now!" Kenny almost screamed.

"Okay, but I need you kids soon—so hurry up."

When Kenny turned back to Laurie he was trying to get hold of himself. "All right," he said to her. "What do you want me to do? Just walk over to everyone and say, 'Sorry, folks, the show's off'?"

"I don't know what to do," Laurie said miserably.

"I don't believe this is happening to me." He had his face in his hands.

Laurie hated herself for the hurt he was feeling. "Do you want *me* to tell everyone?" she asked gently.

He looked at her then, pleading when he heard her tenderness: "Laurie, for God's sake think of what you're doing!"

"Oh believe me, Kenny, I've thought about it a lot!"

"Then why'd you say you'd marry me in the first place?"

Laurie was silent, the question unanswerable. He looked at her and suddenly realized he hadn't really seen her lately. Where had she been? "Don't tell me there's somebody else," he said, shocked.

She didn't reply; rightly, he took her silence for guilt. Now contempt edged his hurt pride: "Oh, so that's the reason," he said.

"No, that's not the reason." But she still didn't deny it.

"I see, Ken said icily. "Well" okay, you just go along, and I'll take care of everything."

"Kenny, I'm sorry . . ." She bent to kiss his cheek but he pushed her away. There were tears in his eyes. "Just—get out of here, now . . . I'll tell everyone."

She fled, out the side aisle, out of the building, into the little red car and onto Hollywood Boulevard. It was twelve thirty and the cool weather uncertain, the sky an even, unmoving gray. Her own interior landscape matched it. All the blankness was frightening. She drove home fast, even ran a red light. She hoped Chris would be home to get her phone call.

21.

The phone was ringing when she got to her apartment. Laurie opened the door and made a dive for the bed, where the phone was half hidden amid the rumpled sheets and discarded tissues. She picked up the receiver and lay down, feeling so emotionally drained she wasn't quite sure she could speak. The person on the other end said hello first. It was a man.

"Hello," she answered faintly.

"Is this Laurie?"

"Yes, this is Laurie." She sighed it out, as though admitting something.

"Laurie, this is Charley Nelson." A serious impersonal voice, full of the intent of business.

"Oh hi, Charley," Laurie said more cheerfully, relieved he wasn't a curious friend or relative. "How are you?"

"Uh—I'm fine." He didn't sound conversational. "Uh—Chris asked me to call you," he went on, "and uh—I don't quite know how to say this . . ."

"What?" Laurie sat up, alarmed.

"Look—we've run into a little problem with the movie," he said.

"What kind of problem?"

"Well, the fact is . . ." He paused, audibly uncomfortable. "The fact is that the studio insists on using a blonde."

"*What*?" Laurie was shocked. A blonde *what*, she thought.

"I—we're really sorry," he said. "I guess you know how much Chris wanted you for the part."

"But Charley, didn't he fight for me? I mean, didn't he tell them he wanted me for the part? I mean, *he's* the director. . . ."

Laurie wondered if she sounded as hysterical as she thought she did.

"I'm sure he did what he could." Charley sounded in command now, his voice had evened to a Hollywood purr.

Laurie felt seriously dizzy and nauseated. She hung her head between her knees, taking the receiver with her. "Where is he now—where's Chris now, Charley?" she mumbled.

"Chris? Oh—he's tied up in a meeting. . . ."

"Why didn't he call me himself?"

"He's at the studio. . . . He thought you ought to know right away."

She straightened up; the horizon settled. "Oh I see. Well thank you, Charley."

"Yeah," he said.

She hung up.

She discovered she was trembling. Feelings of betrayal and disappointment chilled her. She got a sweater. She didn't know what to do next. She picked up the phone again and dialed, then hung up, then dialed the number again.

"Chris Nolan's office, please," she said woodenly.

"Just one moment, I'll connect you."

Laurie thought of connections, all kinds of connections while the phone was ringing. But it was Barbara who answered. "Chris Nolan's office, may I help you?"

"Barbara, hello, this is Laurie—Laurie Robinson," she added. Formalities helped control. "Is Chris there, please?"

"Oh hi, Laurie—why no, he's not. He's at home, I just spoke to him. You know the number?"

"But Charley said he . . . You mean he's not there at a meeting?"

"No, I'm the only sucker working on Saturday," Barbara joked. "He has no scheduled production meetings till next week."

"Oh," Laurie was stunned. "Well okay, thanks, Barbara."

"You want his home number?"

"No, I've got it, thanks," she said again. She heard Barbara saying goodbye as she settled the receiver.

Laurie blew her nose in a half-used tissue and then sat for a minute staring at the pinpoint of

143

light that was the sun's reflection on her empty juice glass, staring straight into it until she forced herself away from the blindness it induced, the inertia. It was clear he had lied; it was clearer she'd been fucked over. How she wanted to run, to escape, to die. But she picked herself up, went to the mirror and looked once at her face, which looked awful. She washed it, then grabbed her bag and stuffed what she would need for the Kiddie Komedy taping on top of Larry.

A few seconds later she was in the elevator. The day attendant was right outside as she emerged running. He greeted her retreating back but she didn't hear him. She was singing to herself to keep from screaming.

22.

Because of the bad weather the retreat from the beach was everywhere around her. Couples predominated, mostly necking in stalled traffic with their bathing suits on. Laurie felt lonely because she was going the other way and was overdressed, although she was only wearing a blouse and skirt. She thought Si was probably trying to call her. *Probably they all are,* she thought. But she didn't care. She asked herself, as the lights changed regularly and the traffic stood still, what she did care about now. Nothing stood up to be counted. Music seemed only to bring pain. "You light up my days and fill my nights . . ." She started to cry but stopped when a man looked with alarm at her contorted face.

It was three in the afternoon by the time she arrived at Chris's house, and the street was as silent and deserted as if everyone were gone or taking a siesta. The house itself looked unoccupied.

At the front door she searched for a doorbell, she hadn't noticed one her other two visits since it had been dark, and he'd had keys. There was a difference to coming here now, she felt. The other night, after they'd made the tape, she had felt almost at home when they'd arrived; now she felt like an intruder.

She found the bell and pushed. Chimes rang somewhere inside and then laughter echoed them and was repeated in another tone. There were people; they came closer.

When Chris pulled open the door his expression of surprise was repeated three times behind him. In the hallway, with handbags and briefcases and obviously on their way *out*, were Carla Wright, Charley Nelson, and a man Laurie knew only as Ed, one of the engineers.

Chris paled, then reddened under his tan. "What are you doing here?" escaped him before he could check his words. He knew he had insulted her, but he was just as confused as she. He was holding his car keys.

"Hi, Laurie," Carla trilled from the hallway. She was drunk and trying not to show it. She hadn't succeeded.

Laurie stared at her over Chris's shoulder, then she looked at Charley, who was a coward and had turned away to talk to Ed rather than face her. She looked back to Chris, to read his eyes, but he was looking at the ground, as if wishing to be swallowed. Something exploded in Laurie's mind; later she thought it had been all her illusions, but suddenly she felt herself burning with anger. Never before had she felt so used.

"I guess this is a bad time," she said in a shaking voice. "I'll speak to you later." She turned to go.

Chris stood tongue-tied. He couldn't say a word with Carla there. Nor did he want to. Carla was someone he needed from time to time. Her beauty flattered him. But he felt he had to say something. "We're all on our way out," he said, taking Laurie's arm. And then in a low, almost surreptitious voice: "Are you all right?"

"Oh I'm just fine!" Laurie said loudly, pulling away from him. "I was just—in the neighborhood, you know, so I—came over to say thanks for helping me with my—uh—act. . . ." It was too hard to keep up. She began walking down the flagstone path.

He caught up with her. There was a hint of concern, perhaps it was guilt, in his tone. "Are you sure you're all right?"

She stopped walking. "Do you think I could—talk to you for a minute? Just one lousy minute so you could explain . . ."

"I can't now, Laurie," he said. "I told you, we're on our way out. . . ."

Out of the corner of her eye Laurie could see the doorway of the house, where beautiful Carla lounged watching them, all arms and legs and

147

casual interest. *I hate her,* Laurie thought. Charley and Ed had disappeared.

"Listen, Laurie—"

I hate him too. "I've got to go," she said. "Maybe I'll talk to you later."

"No wait—" Chris turned and tossing his keys, yelled to Carla. "Here—I'll meet you in the garage, I'm going to walk Laurie to her car."

It was the intimacy of that gesture that made everything clear to Laurie. When he reached for her arm she backed away and put her hand up as if to ward off his touch. "No, wait a minute— don't. No. Don't you walk me anywhere."

23.

She thought she would make it on time even if she stopped. She had to stop. She pulled off the road into a vacant square of asphalt, the lot in front of a diner that was closed, and parked under a tree. More than anything, she didn't want to do Kiddie Komedy today. To do comedy you had to feel expansive, to be open and flexible; Laurie felt the opposite. Guilty and knotted with anger at herself. No one had told her to go home with Chris that night. Why had she done it? What had possessed her? Look what happened! What could possibly have made her do all this? She remembered how Manny used to pull her pigtails and when she turned on him, furious, he would say, mock-innocent: "The devil made me do it!"

"The devil made me do it," she said to the gray sky. "The devil." Then she cried for a long time, wild loud sobs, until suddenly she could hear herself crying, became self-conscious about it, and stopped.

"Oh my god, the show. Poor Si." He was probably pacing the floor, frantic, phoning her every five minutes. She started the car and sped onto the freeway.

But it was Tom she encountered first, blocking the door of the dressing room. "You're late." He was chubby and petulant.

"Yes, I know," Laurie said, stiff as a board. "Look—I'm sorry, excuse me, Tom. I've got to change."

"I don't want to throw you," he said right off without moving, "but the network has the parents sitting with the kids tonight. They're calling it the Family Komedy Hour."

"I do a kid's show, Tom," Laurie said, shocked. Her lip trembled a little.

He relented then. "I'm sorry, Laurie," he said. "But what can I do? They insisted."

"Oh, it's all right, what's the difference anyway," she said, exasperated. "Will you please let me get in to change?"

He moved.

She was in the middle of dressing when Si arrived; having just come from Nussbaum's he stood and stared at her in mute sorrow and disapproval. Still he was in her corner. He loved her, she knew, even if he didn't always agreed with what was right for her. And he didn't say a word, but merely helped her with the overall straps, told her to break a leg, and went to sit in the bleachers with the audience. Laurie saw him when she came out, sitting next to a pretty woman with two small girls. The lech.

"Hi everybody! This is Larry—isn't he cute? Don't applaud too loud he'll start asking for food!" There were a cople of delicate titters in the crowd, but that was all. Laurie settled herself on the stool. She had begun to feel numb. It wasn't going to be easy.

"But seriously, folks, I use my dummy for one compelling reason—he works cheap!"

A loud guffaw. Si.

"Hey listen, I'll have you know this dummy's smart. Why, he finished nursery school in two terms—Nixon's and Ford's. . . . "

Larry wasn't working. She got off the stool and put him on it, he fell forward, grotesquely folded in half. She took the hand mike and walked to the front of the stage to get some eye contact, to involve them, all the while thinking of ad libs. "You know, ladies and gentlemen, I'm gonna do something now I don't usually do at a cheap show like this. . . ."

She waited, no laughter, she walked backstage toward the barnyard backdrop with its mute painted cow, then walked toward the audience again. "I've got a surprise for you folks, I'm going to bring out—my daughter Laurie . . . Laurie Robinson!"

It was Si's old father-daughter act. Laurie glanced left at an imaginary presence. "C'mon kid, don't be shy, c'mon out here . . . Ah, look at her, ain't she beautiful? What a mug!"

They followed her gestures but didn't laugh. Damn them! she thought. "Hey yutz—laugh, willya!" she shouted. "You want me to look bad in front of the kid?"

But they wouldn't even when urged to. She hated them. She spotted a kid scowling in the front row and went directly to him. "You know, you could pose for the label on an iodine bottle— or stand outside a doctor's office to make people sick . . . " She glared at him. He got frightened and seemed to shrink.

She stopped then, as she felt the dead air all around her, and tried to combat the panic she could feel tearing through her body. Tears pressed at her throat. "Hey wow, you know my agent told me this act's a real sleeper . . ." Her voice wobbled dangerously.

She saw Si, anxious, pain on his face.

Gently, correctly, she put the mike back on the stand. "Ladies and gentlemen—I'm sorry. I can't go on. . . ."

Si's footsteps echoed from the bleachers. He got to the dressing room right behind her. Laurie collapsed over the table. He pulled up a chair and leaned over her, stroking her back, patting her like the poor baby they both knew she was at that moment.

"Hey, they were really pretty rough out there tonight," he said gently. "But you'll get 'em."

He was starting again. "I don't want to get them, Si."

"Oh c'mon, sweetie—I know how you feel . . . and that stuff—" he hesitated. "All that stuff with Ken is bothering you, I know."

His disapproval was there, somewhere. "I don't want to talk about it right now," she said.

"Okay, okay, but listen, Laur . . . About the show, it goes back to that old thing, timing . . . "

"Will you stop it! Will you please just stop it!" She sprang from the chair, feeling suffocated, desperate to get out from under his advice and sympathy. "Si, I'm not doing the show anymore—understand? I hate it! I thought I would get to like it, and bear with it because of the money. But I *hate* it! And once and for all—*I'm not funny!*" She was shrieking.

"Aw, c'mon, Laur, shh. . . ." Si stood abject, wounded.

She sighed and sat down, but felt calmer now that she'd yelled at him. Everything seemed easier if she just kept repeating it out loud. "I'm not funny, Si. You are. I'm not."

He was silent. He was admitting it.

But there was her pride, after all. She wanted to make him see that she wasn't altogether lost because of not being able to do what he thought she should do, or what Kenny had wanted her to do. Or what the Fenwick Farms director wanted me to do, she thought. She stood up and started unhooking her overalls.

"Look Si, I'm a good singer, and I'm a good songwriter. There's things I can do."

"You think you're ready to make it that way? What about money?"

"Pop—have you ever even heard my songs?"

"Well not in a while—you know, Laur, I hate to hang around . . ."

She reached in her bag and brought out a copy of the tape she had made with Chris. "This is me, Pop," she said.

He stared at the cassette in his hand, a bit ashamed.

"Don't worry, I'm good." Laurie smiled.

"So what are you gonna do now?" He leaned back in his chair, wearily she noticed. She felt bad that she was tiring him when he needed to take things easy.

"Do you remember that Columbia offer? The one I got just after I got engaged to Ken?"

"No," he confessed. He must have shut that out too.

"They wanted to record me in their studios in New York. And I didn't go. . . ."

Si nodded, thinking.

"So we'll go now," he said. "We'll go back to New York together. I'll work the hills, and you can make records, or whatever . . ."

Oh no. She couldn't believe he was ready to do that, but she didn't know what to say to him either. She went behind the screen and slid out of the Farmer Girl outfit, thankful to be taking it off for the last time. "Look Si—I love you," she began, " . . . and I don't want to hurt you. . . . "

There was silence on the other side of the screen.

" . . . but you've got to let go."

"I didn't know I was holding on." She could almost hear his defensive shrug.

"I'm going to New York alone," Laurie said, and came to that final decision right then. As she said it she realized it was the best idea she'd had in a long time. "Why don't you listen to the tape," she suggested, to cover the uncomfortable silence that followed. She took the cassette from him and slid it into the small recorder she usually carried.

"So many nights I'd sit by my window
Waiting for someone to sing me his song.
So many dreams I kept deep inside me . . . " *

He heard the whole thing through while she finished dressing. When the tape shut off he pulled out the cassette and handed it to her. He didn't say anything, but he was impressed, she could tell.

"Oh, Pop, I love you," Laurie said. She hugged him, kissed his familiar, rough-bearded cheek, and promised to call him as soon as she could. Then she stuffed the tape recorder into her bag on top of Larry, and went out into the hall. The studio was very still. Mercifully, Tom, as well as

* Copyright © 1977 by Big Hill Music Company

the audience, had gone home. There was no one in the half-dark lot either, and it was raining.

By midnight she had made the necessary arragements. Jesse was calling Columbia on Monday. Si's cousin Diane in Queens had offered temporary room and board. Annie would take the piano, or Richard would take the apartment with the piano still in it, whichever, depending on whether Ward and his wife Fran wanted to get rid of their apartment and move into Richard's.

Laurie packed. She slept. She woke up and drank juice and ate vitamins. She played a little tune on the piano, a classical piece Manny had taught her, and then gently closed the lid. Then she got into the elevator with the two suitcases that contained all her priceless possessions.

The elevator stopped at the ninth floor and there stood the day attendant, in the middle of an enormous yawn. Laurie grinned. When he recovered himself and got in with her he was shaking his head and laughing. He carried her suitcases to the car and checked the oil for her, which was down one quart.

"You're going to New York in this?" he said. Dubiously.

She nodded. She had it all set up: the maps, etc., and even the tape recorder on the front seat beside her.

He shrugged, gave the fender a pat, and stood back to let her pass. "Take care of the ninth floor," she teased on her way out, and left him laughing.

One block later, on Sunset Boulevard, Laurie caught a glimpse of herself in the rear-view mirror. She had a big smile on her face too, one that broadened, she noticed, when she got to the freeway and took the entrance marked East. The hills of San Bernadino appeared, gray in the distance; above them rose the early morning sun. She stretched a little, put a cassette in the recorder, and stepped on the gas.

It's the morning of my life,
I want to write you a song.
It's the start of something nice,
And so I'll write you a song.
I'll paint it rainbows and dreams.
Looking for love in the city
And make believing that life is real.
Looking for someone who's pretty.
It's the morning of my life,
And so I'll write you a song.
It's the morning of my life, and so I'll write
you a song.*

Bestselling Novels from POCKET BOOKS

_____ 81785 A BOOK OF COMMON PRAYER Joan Didion $1.95

_____ 81685 CATCH A FALLING SPY Len Deighton $1.95

_____ 82352 THE CRASH OF '79 Paul E. Erdman $2.75

_____ 80720 CURTAIN Agatha Christie $1.95

_____ 81806 THE INVESTIGATION Dorothy Uhnak $2.50

_____ 81207 JOURNEY Marta Randall $1.95

_____ 82340 THE LONELY LADY Harold Robbins $2.75

_____ 81881 LOOKING FOR MR. GOODBAR Judith Rossner $2.50

_____ 82446 LOVERS AND TYRANTS Francine Du Plessix Gray $2.25

_____ 80986 THE NAVIGATOR Morris West $2.50

_____ 81378 OVERBOARD Hank Searls $1.95

_____ 80938 PLAGUE SHIP Frank G. Slaughter $1.95

_____ 81036 PURITY'S PASSION Janette Seymour $1.95

_____ 81644 THE STARMAKER Henry Denker $2.50

_____ 81135 THE TARTAR Franklin Proud $2.50

POCKET BOOKS
Department FB 6-78
1230 Avenue of the Americas
New York, N.Y. 10020

Please send me the books I have checked above. I am enclosing
$_____ (please add 50¢ to cover postage and handling for each
order; N.Y.S. and N.Y.C. residents please add appropriate sales tax). Send
check or money order—no cash, stamps, or C.O.D.'s please. Allow up to
six weeks for delivery.

NAME_____

ADDRESS_____

CITY_____ STATE/ZIP_____

FB 6-78